I0691381

USN COMPANY 209

First Edition

Published by The Nazca Plains Corporation
Las Vegas, Nevada
2010

ISBN: 978-1-935509-93-6
Ebook: 978-1-61098-010-4

Published by

The Nazca Plains Corporation ®
4640 Paradise Rd, Suite 141
Las Vegas NV 89109-8000

PUBLISHER'S NOTE
USN Company 209 is a work of fiction created wholly by *El Aurens'* imagination. All characters are fictional and any resemblance to any persons living or deceased is purely by accident. No portion of this book reflects any real person or events.

Male Cover Photo, Konrad Bak
Ship Photo, Nicole Waring

Art Director,
Blake Stephens

DEDICATION

This is dedicated to my dearest friends for their love and acceptance of me for who I am: Angel, Caesar, Carla, Connie, Daisy, Jannie, "Nubi," "Prince," Sally, "Spunkie," and Scott.

My sincere thanks go to Jerry, Bill, Drew, and especially to Tommy, Hank, and Chuck for all the time and effort they spent in trying to help me improve.

And a very special dedication in loving remembrance of JASON and NICKY, and of HANK S. They know why. May they ever look over my shoulders and continually inspire me to do better.

Allez avec Dieu, mes amis.
Vaya con Dios, mis amigos.
يذهب مع الله ، أوأصدقائي
Go with God, my friends.
There is only One, known by many names.

USN COMPANY 209

First Edition

El Aurens

CONTENTS

CONTENTS CONTINUED...

AUTHOR'S NOTE

As I began this exercise of writing in 2nd Person Narrative — "you, you, your, yours" — it became the most exciting story I'd ever begun. Most of my writing has been in 3rd Person Narrative — "he, she, it; him, her, it; his, her, hers, its; they, them, their, theirs". Wow, what a list. An occasional story of mine has been in 1st Person Narrative — "I, me, my, mine." Each author has his own favorite.

I'd never written in 2nd Person Narrative before, but, instead of a frown on my brow, it pulled a smile across my face as it unfolded. Re-edit after re-edit, and I still found errors. I'm not perfect by any means, but it was fun.

Oh. My grammar... if any of the authors I edit/proof-read for were to scribe like this little ribaldry is written, I'd skin 'em alive. But the apparent errors are done intentionally. I swear by all that's holy. The main character is a country-boy, high-school educated, and CAN speak Standard American English, though he's more comfortable with his deep, ingrained, multi-syllabic Southe'n drawl. The same applies to the narrator of the story, who, being so enamored with the young man, falls into a similar brogue, himself. Each sometimes uses both within the same paragraph — but then... WHO thinks about paragraphs when he's talking or thinking? Screw the *polite language and the use of exclamation points; I'll say it like it is! "I swear I'm tellin' tha truth, tha whole truth, an' nuthin' but tha truth, so he'p me, Jehoshaphat!"*

So, on with the story. Turn off the TV. Turn off your cell phone. Turn off the porn site you've been watching on the computer. Let the dog out. Get a good brewski or tall bottle of water, and set it nearby. You'll want to sit up straight (no pun intended), feet no more than six inches apart and with both flat on the floor. This IS a military story, you know. Get into character. Let nothing, but nothing, disturb your concentration or attention; and have your hand ever on the ready to diddle with your little... errr...pencil or highlighter?

Oh, well. Forwarrrrd... HUT!

CHAPTER ONE

Goodbye, Okefenokee. Hello, Red.

You're eighteen years old, TODAY — more than a half century ago, that is. But in yesteryear's TODAY, it wasn't many weeks ago that you, with great joy, graduated from a back-country little red schoolhouse. You're reminiscing, staring into the sky, dotted hither and yon with fluffy white cotton bolls of clouds. You're gently swaying in your weathered, wooden hammock, homemade from barrel-staves. It's strung out between two Long Needle Pines in the Georgia portion of Okefenokee Swamp — your favorite spot in the whole world... or what you'd seen of it, anyway. With the Gators and Bobcats and Eastern Diamondback Rattlers and Cottonmouth Water Moccasins, it's still all you've ever known. It's a good life, a simple life, where you were raised as a young'un.

As said, you're a young man in that long ago TODAY. In some parts of this great nation of ours, you were considered old enough to offer your life in sacrifice for your country, if needed in time of war, but not old enough to vote; it didn't seem fair. Ya coulda become fodder for foreign or friendly fire, butcha couldn't walk into a bar or a saloon and order a simple bottle o' beer, much less a bourbon-on-the-rocks, or a splash of J&B. And they didn't have moonshine or hooch or white lightnin'... at least not so's any revenuer could see when he wandered in.

You'd never smoked a cigarette… well, again, not so's anybody in the family would know, but you'd always enjoyed watchin' your granddaddy an' uncles an' older cousins roll their own from the dried, flue-cured tobacca in the family's barns. You always loved the sweet, astringent fragrances o' different pipe and cigar tobaccas, though the mere thought of snuff and chawin' tabacky made you sicker'n a 'coon to your stomach.

Your step-daddy's mama's teeth were yeller and brown — those that were still left in her mouth — and rotting, it seemed. Ya reckon her bein' your step-daddy's mama made her your "step-gran'mama"? Humph. Ya hated for her to kiss ya good-night. Or good-mornin'. Or any other time, for that matter. Her breath? Oh, God, it was atrocious with that chaw between her gum and her right cheek, and a dip o' snuff liquefyin' and droolin' from the left corner of her partially blackened lips. She was addicted to the homegrown stuff. Ya knew that soon, she'd plop her fat ass in her army-blanket-covered rockin' chair in the main room for the rest of the evenin' and use the fetid ol' spittoon on the floor nearby. Ya sure hoped she wouldn't miss it again; ya hated havin' to clean that shit up, down on your knees with your be-hind stuck up in the air.

Or maybe you'd hear her get up and open the squeaky screen door and spit outside, the ol' 'coon-dog on the porch yelpin' in surprise at the smelly splash on his hind-end in the dark o' the night. Cooter was a good ol' hound-dog, though. Ya miss him, don'tcha? Yeah, I know you do. He was a pal to ya, all those years ago before you left and later came home to find that havin' arthritis, he'd been too slow ta git outta the way and was run over by the tractor when your step-daddy was plowin' up the field after the cotton had been picked. Instead o' pushin' up daisies, ya reckoned that his sweet ol' remains would be pushin' up some more cotton tha next year. Maybe some o' that light brown strain of cotton — a rare, but not uncommon throwback. In school, you found a book that said that colored cottons grew in small quantities all around the world — ecru, mauve, green, red, golden brown, and chocolate brown, but all of'em could be found in Peru. Maybe something in Cooter's fur would transfer his color into the cotton plants whose roots would reach down into his tilled and decaying dead body.

He loved ya, ol' Cooter did, in a huntin'-dog sorta way, always bringin' ya gifts of dead rats or baby raccoons or tha little red fox he went 'n' caught, still clingin' to life, the little critter was.

Ah, well, back to the present yesteryear. Soon enough, all that you'd ever been familiar with in the past would be behind you. Ya always wanted to leave the family nest; ya never 'zactly felt like you was one of'em. Nosireeebobolinski.

The day before you were to leave and when the sun was at its highest, ya went across the bay in your rough-hewn cypress canoe — yep; tha folks that lived there in Okefenokee called the waterways, *bays,* jes like tha folks down in Mississip an' Lusiana had their own *bayous.* Ya wanted to say *goo'-bye* to Shadrach and Vashti, friends o' your step-daddy's, but more importantly, ya wanted to see Darkness one more time afore ya left. He was Shad and Vashti's strappin' boy, the same age as you; in fact, you and he shared the very same birthday.

You two boys had grown up together, notwithstandin' your differences. On those few-and-far-between times when your mama and his were avisitin', you little guys cooed an' giggled to each other as you crawled around in your innocent nakedness on the dirt floor of either of your shacks, playin' with the simplest of home-made toys. And when you got tired, you'd wrap your little nude bodies around or across each other, satisfying some primal need that neither you nor your mamas could understand. Maybe you'd suck your own thumbs; maybe you'd suck each other's; it made no difference to you so long as your chests, arms, and legs touched the warmth and softness of the other's body, black or white.

Shad and your step-daddy occasionally worked together in the fields and in the swamp itself. Vashti and your mama would often share some of the food they'd each grown, or the meat the men-folk had butchered — gator, snake, turtle, rabbit, squirrel, or the best of'em all… wild turkey.

Then, bein' as they were your only neighbors for miles around, you and Darkness were sorta forced together from the time y'all were itty-bitty babies, even though you were as white as the inside of an uncooked tater, and he was as black as a sweet, juicy prune. You'd been told that right after you were born, your mama took sick, an' your step-daddy gave you to Vashti an' Shad to take care of until your mama got better.

That was *some* sight — seein' Darkness suckle one of Vashti's black teats while occasionally, but at the same time, your pink lips suckled the other one. It was like you were supposed to be twins. Your souls surely touched each other in ways that nobody understood… at least, not in that day and age of racial discrimination, but your mama was sick, and Vashti was actin' as your wetnurse.

In your pre-teen years, you both began to show your strong independence from your families. You began discovering things and exploring Okefenok beyond the livable areas around your homes. Ya hiked where ya could, or rowed your dugouts over the bays to areas that the grownups had probably never seen.

But that day when ya went to say *goo'bye*, Vashti had known you were coming over and had prepared lunch for you boys. When you arrived at their humble abode, the first thing you noticed was a slightly familiar wild, gamey, but not-so-enjoyable fragrance wafting through the open doorway.

Soon, you and Darkness were sitting at the makeshift table with dried-out, old tree stumps for seats. Vashti brought over two chipped-enameled deep-dishes of the fragrant soup... a yellow one for you and a blue one for Darkness. Then she brought over a plate of steamin', right-out-of-the-skillet homemade yellow cornbread for dunkin' in that spicy, hot soup, and a small plate of watercress salad sprinkled with wild cranberries and chopped hickory nutmeats with a wild-honey-and-mustard dressing.

"That what I think it is?" you asked, the question being directed to Vashti.

With the heavy accent you'd heard all your life, she answered, "It be Kuta."

Before she could say more, Darkness jumped up from his seat and darted over to a corner of the shack, picked up something, and whirled around, showing you the top half of a black, brown, and yellow turtle shell, its inner side still soft from having the meat recently removed. Black ants were already beginning to crawl around, pincering the shell clean of the soon-to-be-rotting remnants of meat that were still attached to the shell.

"*COOTER!*" you exclaimed with excitement. Never had you seen such a large turtle shell before... about eighteen inches across from side to side.

It had been another 'cooter' that had given name to the yelpin' hound-dog puppy that brought home a young snappin'-turtle clamped to its lower lip years earlier. You smiled at the memory.

"*KUTA!*" Vashti emphasized.   "*Afrique.*   Malinké word of Mandinka," she grinned, quickly nodding her head. "Eat. Eat," she encouraged. "Taste be bettah th'n smell." At that, she wrinkled up her nose as she also rubbed her tummy.

And she was right. The Kuta Soup was delicious with it's wild onions, garlic, and radishes, despite nearly having to hold your nose while you ate it.

When you and Darkness had finished eating, you got up and gave Vashti a hug and a kiss on the cheek. "Thanks, *Maman,*" you said, using the name that Darkness had always called his mother. And then, quick as a flash, lickety-split, you eighteen-year-olds were out the doorway and gone. In your separate dugouts and across the bays, you rowed to a spot that was special to you both — a little crescent-shaped island with a cove where those adorable gentle giants, the Manatees, gathered and nibbled on their own vegetarian lunches of the aquatic plants that grow underwater, of the floating water lilies, and of the all-purpose cattail.

Beaching the dugouts, you both hurriedly stripped off your overalls — as you always did — and, naked as jay-birds, dove into the crystal-clear water. For some reason, the gators 'n' moccasins never seemed to bother the Manatees, so you weren't afraid to go in the water. Five of the clumsy, slow-moving giants were there, along with two little ones who were more interested in nursing than in nibbling the grasses.

You and Darkness swam among the friendly, sometimes-called, sea cows rubbing their sides, their cheeks, and their heads; they'd even let you ride on their backs as they gently paddled through the water that was no more than four feet at its deepest in the cove.

Never having more than five or six teeth, they used their flexible prehensile upper lip to grab leaves and other parts of plants, then, like it was an elephant's trunk, they would push the leafy foodstuffs into their mouths to be chewed by the few teeth in the rear.

As Darkness was atop the back of one of the Manatees, another came up and began grabbing at his black toes with its prehensile lip. Ya'd never heard him scream so loud before. You stood there in the water that was up to your nipples, and yet another Manatee came over to you and grabbed at your own flaccid dick that was idly waving in the movement of the surrounding water. Talk about hollerin', and jumpin', and runnin' up onto the little grassy beach! Woulda thought you were a frightened girl-child. Hahahahaha. Oh, Lordy, me!

But soon, you were back in their world, swimmin' as normal, and playin' tag under water with each other, and with the adult Manatees as well as the babies.

There was a bit of grab-assin' goin' on between you guys, pinchin' and squeezin' butt-cheeks, and balls, and once… just out of curiosity… you wraped your hand 'round Darkness' black shaft of hooded man-meat, felt it throb, and quickly removed your hand.

After about an hour or so of being in the water, you both tired a little, got out, and stretched yourselves on the soft grasses of the island, on your backs, within arm's length of each other. With no wind about, the sun soon became hot, and your bodies dried of the swamp water. Then Nature took over and — black AND white — your bodies began to glisten with droplets of sweat. Not perspiration. Sweat. Country-boys' SWEAT!

Darkness turned his head to the right and looked at you. You sensed the movement, turned your head, and looked at him.

"Ya ready ta leave tamarra?" he asked. His voice was kinda sad, kinda solemn at the same time.

"I guess," you answered. Then after a minute, you said, "Gonna miss ya."

"Gonna miss ya, too."

"Ya been like a brother ta me… since tha day we was born."

"Ya be like one ta me, too, ya know?" he asked.

You noticed a bead of sweat begin to roll off his right pec and down toward his rippled abs. You turned over onto your left side and propped yourself up on your elbow. Then, without thinking, you swiped your hand across that glistening black skin and wiped away the trickling sweat. Seeing something else, you grinned and stuck the end of your pointer-finger into the little well of his bellybutton, and jiggled it around, making the puddle of sweat slosh out and down the side of his hip. His dick jumped a tad, and you saw it plump up a bit. That caused your own to jerk slightly, and you felt a drop of that slick, shiny, sweet-tastin' stuff land on your left thigh, but you didn't know what it was rightly called. You'd tasted your own a few times, but you wouldn't think o' tastin' anybody else's, not even the juice drippin' from Darkness' dick.

He must have seen the movement, too, 'cause he rolled over on his right side and propped himself up on his elbow. "Can I touch you like you be touchin' me?" he asked with wide eyes and raised eyebrows.

You nodded in assent. He smiled and timidly licked his sun-dried lips. Ever so cautiously, he placed his left hand over your entire right pec and moved it in a small circular motion. The hot, almost-white palm of his big black hand sent tingles through your hard, sensitive nipple. You squeezed your eyes shut, and moaned aloud as your dick jumped to full attention, though by being on your side, it dangled toward the ground a bit.

Darkness slid his hand down your sweat-slick chest, ran the tips of his fingers through your blond pubic hair, and suddenly froze... almost terrified.

Your eyes flew open. "WHAT?" you asked.

A moment's hesitation. He slowly withdrew his hand and rolled off his side onto his back again as he looked out at the ripples in the water caused by the playing of the Manatees.

"WHAT?" you repeated the question.

He answered, but it was all mumbled.

"Sumpin's wrong; now, what is it, Darkness?" you asked, sitting up so you could look straight down into his unsmiling, almost fearful, face.

He looked away from your eyes, out to the left and, with hesitation between the words, said, "We'uns cain't do this."

"Do what?"

"Tetch each uther like we wuz doin'."

"We've touched each other before — lots o' times," you shot back.

"But not nekkid, an' not down there," he said, turning back his head and looking at your deflating cock.

You were still in a playful mood and threw yourself, full-body, on top of Darkness, your once-again inflating cock next to his, your bellies and chests against each other, your hard nipples pressing against his, and your noses tip to tip. You wanted so much to kiss those thick, juicy, black lips of his, but didn't dare to make the move. He grappled with you, trying to get away, but you grabbed his wrists and held them to the ground above his head. "Lemme tell ya sumpin', brother. When I wuz in school, I had to read *The Knight's Tale* from Geoffrey Chaucer's *Canterbury Tales*…"

He crossed his eyes and gave you the dumbest look ever, 'cause he didn't understand a word you wuz sayin'. But you went on as you had, many times, tryin' to give him some learnin'.

"…an' to the best o' my recollection, he wrote sumpin' like this: 'All that night, the Greeks did play the games I care not to say who, *NAKED*, and with oil anointed, did wrastle best.'

"Huh?" was all he could say.

"I seen pictures of them people hundreds and hundreds of years ago. They wore mighty *fine* white clothes trimmed in red and purple and gold all the time, but when they were sportin', like we do when we go skinny-dippin', they wuz nekkid. And when they wuz wrastlin', I seen pictures of'em with big prongs like we got right now." You lifted your hips a bit, released one of his wrists, and grabbed hold of his AND your dicks, with one hand, and stroked 'em a couple of times; then you lay back down on top of him, that slick, shiny goo oozin' from both cock-hoods onto your bellies. "So, if the smartest and most powerful men back then could wrastle nekkid, I reckon we can do it, too," you finished your lecture, smiling and grinding your slimy pricks together; it felt so good.

Darkness looked into your eyes. It felt like he was tryin' to get into your very soul. Suddenly, the thought flew through your mind, 'He's usin' what VooDoo powers his mama gave…'

But he broke your thought by asking, "Is you on top o' me 'cause you be a white boy an' I be a darkie? Is you wantin' t'be tha Mastah an' me tha slave?"

Shocked at his question, you jerked back into an upright position. "Where tha fuck did *that* come from, Darkness? We're not master an' slave; we're *brothers*; don'tcha know that? Whatcha talkin' 'bout?" you asked.

THEN, you felt *his* monster throb beneath your ass-crack, and his white teeth were brilliant between his grinning lips. "In that case... *brutha...*" he said.

In an instant, you found yourself tossed flat on your back. Darkness sat astride your hips and jacked *both* dicks with one bigger, thicker, stronger hand, the other one on your chest, holding you down as he twisted and squeezed your right nipple.

"I be wantin' t'do this ever since we started shootin' off together when you said we wuz becomin' men."

Your mama (only in the biological sense, ya rightly know) took ya to tha Recruiter's office on the edge of Atlanna, in the ol' rattley pick-up, spewin' exhaust smoke and irritatin' ever'body behind her. Not wantin' ya to be the laughin' stock o' the family, she letcha wear your newest and best sea-blue bib overalls, even though they was a couple sizes too small, a couple shades too light from bleaching all the pig-slop 'n' hog-shit outta your knees durin' washin' days, and a little too tight for your own good. Ya'd gotten'em, brand-spankin'-new three Christmases ago. Beneath, were yer scruffy ol' sockless clodhoppers... muddy, shitty, and scraped by the barbed-wire ya had to crawl through to catch the little piggies for your step-daddy. He'd toss the li'l squealers in the huge caldron of boilin'-hot water that was outside the kitchen screen door, then skin'em and butcher'em and cure'em for tha best damn bacon anybody ever crunched their teeth on.

"Onest y'all gits yer uni-forms," your mama was tellin' ya in the pick-up, "ya kin jes throw'em in tha sea; they ain't worth nuthin', no-how, and 'sides that, they's gittin' right indecent on ya. Bet you'll soon be havin' lots o' hot, leakin' fillies crawlin' all over that snake hangin' 'tween yer legs."

You jerked your head around so ya could see'er straight-on, and your jaw dropped near down to tha light blond fur on your chest.

"Oh, don't look so s'prised... I done seen it since ya growed up; a coupla times I did... one mornin' I went to gitcha outta bed, 'n' when I went in your room, ya'd kicked the sheet off, and there 'twere! Stickin' straight up like a juicy fuckin' flagpole. If 'tweren't so ungodly-like..." she grinned atcha and wriggled her eyebrows, "... I'd've given it a quick tryout a few times… but don'tcha go tellin' narry a soul what I done went 'n' said; ya heah, ya son-of-a-bitch; ya heah me?" she asked as she slapped your face… one… more… time. She had a habit of doin' that: joshin' ya and then slappin' ya if she thought you were gonna tell anyone what she said. An' ya doubted the tub-o'-lard she'd become even realized she was referrin' to herself when she called you a son-of-a-bitch!

"Yes'am." Ya weren't scared of her, butcha knew that a gen'leman neva strikes a lady, no matter how un-lady-like she seems. It says so right in the Bible — or at least that's what she'd done learned ya.

Then, after talkin' to that real nice-lookin' recruiter hisself, an' signin' all the paperwork, ya got a coupla travel chits from'im, an' after sayin' bye to your mama — without kissin' her and without ever lookin' back — you took the city bus out to the airport. Ya found a flight to Chicago that'd leave in only four hours. Hot damn! You were really and truly, finally, on your way outta that effin', good-fer-nuthin' family. Ya knew that country-folk were the salt o' the earth, butcha felt that your own people were the mud that hides the salt.

For the first time in your life, though — all eighteen years of it — you really felt alone… really alone, but free at last, an' it felt good — no responsibility to anyone but Uncle Sam an' to the Grand Ol' Flag that waved on that tall, tall flagpole out in front of the airport terminal buildin'. Even without your uniform yet, ya saluted the flag with a dog-grin of a smile on your face. Ya were mighty proud to be able, finally, to call yourself a sailor in the Navy of the great U-nited States of America. Very proud. Proud 'nough to know deep down that ya wanted to make a career of… yeah… "ridin' the waves." Heehee. Oh, yeah. Though ya knew in your heart that ya was how-some-ever dif'ernt.

Ya chuckled to yourself visu'lizin' the word, 'Waves', bein' cap'talized when referrin' to the female gender; sailors in skirts, that's what they wuz! It "sounded" good, and ya knew you could say it in front of all the jocks, and muscle-studs, and pussy-pounders, and clit-lickers that ya'd soon be bunkin' in with during Basic Trainin'. Well, not really bunkin' *in* with, but ya knew what it meant. Ya'd seen all them testosterone-filled gods and smelled'em and drooled at the visions of all them nekkid men in the Navy as well as them what was in your own real life — the ones in the locker room and showers after gym class. And — lucky you (wink, wink) — you were the "Manager" of the little high school football team. Yeah!

Those were sommme hunks, weren't they? You also knew that in Navy Basic, there'd be at least four or five times that many nekkid men in the barracks and showers! Whoo-o-oo-eee!

At the mere thought o' all that smelly man-meat and muscle-sweat, ya felt a tingle in your dingle and reached down to give it a couple o' rubs through the faded denim.

Then, thinkin' back to the locker room and showers in high school, you remembered sorta bonin'-up wearin' nothin' but that old ratty jockstrap that looked like it'd never been washed a day in its life, while you were handin' out towels to the drippin', rippled abs and half-hard cocks... errr... jocks... errr... football players. All them athaletes loved ribbin' ya and teasin' ya, and they was the ones that made ya wear that stained, smelly ol' piece o' shit while handin' out the clean towels and doin' all that messy clean-up in the stinkin' hole from hell they called a locker room. But jes' bein' able to be 'round'em made ya love all their *special* a'tention. Like rubbin' their smelly tri-colored jocks all over your face and head when they was on their way to the showers.

Just like there in the airport, your teenaged boyhood grew larger in your too-small overalls. Several guys, and not jest a few girls in the waitin' area, snickered, pointed, or whispered behind shieldin' fingers. Ya knowed that ya either had to sit down, do some slow deep-breathin' exercises, and redirect your thoughts, or ya had to hurry into a cubical in the men's room, close and lock the damned door, slip your shoulder straps over your buff arms, let them ol' overalls drop to the floor, and take matters in your own hands in order to rid yourself o' some possible leakage and embarrassment. Ya took the former rather than the latter, 'cause the latter'd take longer than tha former. An' ya felt like ya was about to bust a nut, bigger'n the ol' Mississip.

After a few moments of gradual, determinedly-controlled breathin', ya got everything back to its usual flaccid state, gave the area under your blond hairy balls a coupla good scratches, and once again ya was able to get up, walk around, an look in the windows of the shops surroundin' the waitin' area.

Spottin' a tobacca shop — and tobacca bein' tha family's small-scale business (along with cotton and corn) — you went to see how all the bundled aromatic leaves ended up. Ya'd heard a few names: Marlboro (a MAN's cigarette — God! He was a hunk, that man on the roadside billboards!), Camel (Slow down; pleasure up), Lucky Strike (means fine tobacco), Chesterfield (Blow some my way), Winston (tastes good like a cigarette should), L&M (just what the doctor ordered), and Kool (a right nice lady's menthol cigarette, coolin' and soothin' to the palate — maybe makin' it easier for her to take your 'polecat' dick all the way down her femi-nine throat. Jes' maybe! If she was of a mind ta do such a thing). Lordy… a nice girl'd never think o' doin' a thing like that, but a good girl… now, a good girl might do that *if* ya paid her 'nough money. And Lord only knows… don't even think 'bout anotha boy or man doin' something dirty like that! He'd druther kill ya first than do somethin' that nasty. Not that a redneck had any qualms 'bout screwin' or fuckin' a dead asshole… wouldn't be anythin' worse than usin' a knothole in a piece o' lumber, or stickin' his pecker through a hole in the partition in the men's crapper over yonder at Bubba's Fillin' Station out on Old U.S. Hwy. #1.

Oh! Speakin' o' polecats… don't that jes' make ya think o' the pitcher-show ya sneaked into one Friday night at tha Bijou? Well, don't it? "Seven Brides for Seven Brothers", with lyrics by Johnny Mercer:

> *I'm a lonesome polecat, lonesome, sad and blue*
> *'Cause I ain't got no femi-nine polecat*
> *Vowin' to be true*
> *Cain't make no vow to a herd of cows.*
> *I'm a mean old hound dog, bayin' at the moon*
> *'Cause I ain't got no lady-friend hound dog*
> *Here to hear my tune*
> *A man cain't sleep when he sleeps with sheep.*
> *I'm a little old hoot owl hootin' in the trees*
> *'Cause I ain't got no little gal owl fowl*
> *Here to shoot the breeze*
> *Cain't shoot no breeze with a bunch of trees.*
> *Why cain't I lose these lonesome polecat blues?*

Why cain'tcha? Well, maybe 'cause… uhhh… well, ya'd find out soon 'nough. Believe you me; ya'd find out sooooon e-nough. Jes' go with the flow and do what comes naturally. That's right… 'c.o.m.e.s.'… But 'c.u.m.s.' is prob'ly right, too. Shucks! It's all good.

Anyways, back to the tobacco shop.

Ya was getting' kinda fidgety and had to find somethin' to do with your hands, so ya broke down an' boughtcha one of them bright red packs of Marlboros. Some folks had said that smokin' relaxes 'n' calms 'em down, so ya decided to give 'em a try. Them times you'd snuck off to the ol' swimmin' hole with a coupla sneaked, hand-rolled cigs, ya'd learned not to cough your foolhardy head off from the first few drags.

Ya asked for a pack of matches from the purtty lady what smelled so good at the counter while ya was openin' the 'Man's Cigarettes'; ya lit up, inhalin' deeply, throwin' your head back, and blowin' the smoke into the air above you. Ya thought that looked so 'mascu-line'.

It was then that a cough exploded from your throat and lungs, causin' ya to double over, your ass stickin' up in the air almost apoppin' outta that tight, slick, shiny backside o' your overalls, coughin' again and again. Ya weren't so used to cigarettes as you thoughtcha was; now was ya? Thank the Good Lord... when ya was doubled over, ya didn't fart, 'cause if ya hada, you'da sure as shootin' split the ass-seam outta them overalls.

A deep, masculine voice asked, "You all right, kid?" as ya felt a hand slappin' your back. Not your 'backside', now, remember. It was too early in his game to be slappin' your 'backside', but it wasn't too late to be slappin' your 'back'.

With a couple more muffled, choked coughs while ya wuz still bent over, ya turned your head, slow-like, and looked right straight into the mounded crotch of some Navy 'whites'. Ya gave a few quick nods as ya slowly stood up, eyes trailin' the front of the guy's white jumper and four-in-hand Navy-blue tie. "Ummmm," ya moaned just before a final cough, and then ya twisted your neck and head as you made a grand swallow of saliva, mucus, smoke, or somethin' like that — maybe a mixture of 'em all.

That ivory-skinned, freckle-faced, red-headed sailor in front of ya, with his 'dog dish' white sailor's cap sittin' askew on his butch-cut, took away all o' your reasonin' power for the moment. He had to be wearin' Fruit-o'-the-Loom whites rather than boxers, the way that crotch filled out them white pants that could hide nothing — not the outline of his briefs against the dimpled cheeks of his smooth, squeezable but-tocks, and not the coppery brillo pad of pubic hair what filled out his tackle even more than his mule dick and bull's balls. <Deep sigh> Ya know that li'l bit of information, *now*, but ya didn't know it *then*. All ya could do was make a supposin' I.D.

"Thank ya, Sir," ya wheezed with a sense of gratitude, your eyes finally finishin' their wanderin' as they focused on his smilin' Irish-green eyes, with what seemed like reflections of heavenly stars in'em. And 'tweren't even noon yet! Ohhh, Lordy!

"For what? And there's no need to call me 'Sir'. I'm just an enlisted man."

Ya shrugged your shoulders, not knowin' why ya'd thanked him. Ya were so cute and funny and innocent and naïve and, yes, embarrassed; your ears and cheeks showed it — they was on their way to turnin' scarlet. But only you knew the reason for your sensitivity; it coulda been any of a hunerd different reasons.

With nerves aflare, ya tried to calm your shakin' hand as ya took another kinder, gentler drag from the manly Marlboro. It went down easy-like, and when ya went to exhale, ya had 'nough courtesy ta keep the fronts o' your lips together while ya blew the smoke outta the corners of your mouth. Ya looked like a railroad engine lettin' off steam in both di-rections at the same time, butchur eyes an' his looked like they was frozen into each other's sight-lines, and it looked like ya both had to think about blinkin', jes' ta git 'nough moisture 'n' sparkle in'em.

Ya slowly reached out your hand ta shake his, and then ya decided ya better put the cig in your other hand before he got burned.

"Peter Dix," ya said softly, "but you can call me 'Pete'," ya said a little more loudly.

He reached out his hand and shook yours. His grip was strong, and it didn't feel like he wanted to let go. "Fred's the name," he said, "but you can call me 'Red'... Red Johnson." He was still holdin' your hand and it didn't feel like he was gonna let go.

Before he could say anything else, your eyes darted up to his red hair, and then, just as quickly, they dropped to his crotch, and ya blushed. Immediately, ya tightly squeezed your eyes shut, telling unspoken volumes as you lit up like a Christmas tree — ya was green around the gills, and your ears was red.

He leaned in closer to ya 'n' whispered, "Yes, Pete… they and little Mister Johnson are as red as what's on top of my head. And please, don't be embarrassed. I've gotten reactions like yours all my life. Well, ever since I sprouted body-hair." He finally let go of your hand. Yours was wet with nervous sweat, butcha didn't know if it was his sweat or yourn. At that moment, ya didn't ever wanna wash that hand again.

"Ya mean…?" ya asked as ya quickly gazed at the red fuzz on Red's arms. And then ya looked back toward his crotch but hurriedly changed your line of vision to his pants-covered thighs and calves.

"Yep," came the answer. "Everything…" he turned completely around like a Sears and Roebuck model or something, "…from the top of my head — the one on my shoulders…" he grinned a wickedly evil broad smile — "…to the edges of my toenails."

"Ummmmmmm," ya quietly moaned, as your very wet tongue unconsciously moistened your lips. Suddenly you looked terrified that you'd spoken or done somethin' too out-o'-turn.

Picking up on your conflicting thoughts and emotions, Red changed the conversation to a more comfortable line. "So, tell me, Pete; where are you from, and where are you headed, a good-lookin' fella like you, and, I guess, all alone here in Atlanta's airport." Pointing to two adjoining empty seats in the waiting area, he added, "Let's go over there and sit down and take a load off."

Ya jerked your head toward'im. "Ya mean… right outchere in front o' God 'n' ever'body?"

Ya both were walkin kinda slow-like, toward the empty seats.

Red scrunched up his eyebrows an' studied ya for a few seconds, prob'ly tryin' to figure out whatcha meant. Finally, it registered, his face relaxed, an' he started laughin' — hilariously!

Ya suddenly stopped walkin', balled up your fists 'n' threw'em onto your hips, then asked loud 'nough for ever'body 'round to hear, "What's so damned cotton-pickin' funny, Red?" Your eyes blazed daggers at'im. "Ya laughin' at me 'cause I'm jesta plain ol' country bumpkin hick?"

Ya sounded really pissed, an' if ya was a pastured bull, ya'd be apawin' at the dirt with snot-spray comin' outta both sides o' your nose, sure as shootin', ya would.

"No, no. I wasn't laughing at you, Pete. Now, come on over here and sit down. I'll tell you what I was laughing at."

Ya walked over, and both of you took a seat. Ya looked at him, with an anger on your face that spoke as loud as words. He looked at you with an adorable grin on his.

"I'm awaitin'," ya said.

"I can tell," he replied.

After an uncomfortably long moment for ya, ya asked, "Well…?"

Red was still grinning, and ya couldn't figure'im out. He moved a little closer, turned a bit, put his left arm around your shoulders, and eased his other hand onto your right thigh.

Ya made no bones about looking down at Red's hand. He squeezed, but nice 'n' slow, not too hard, and then slowly slid his hand just a tad bit closer to your… ya know. The tingle in your dingle began to rise again and ya looked once more into his eyes.

"What I meant when I suggested that we come over here, sit down, and _take_ a load off was to relax and take the weight of your body off your feet. If I'd said to _get_ a load off, I would've meant to 'spank the monkey', or jack-off, or…" Red looked around to see if anyone was listening to them, "…to fuck somebody — woman _or_ man. There's a big difference between _taking_ a load off and _getting_ a load off."

"Oh, my! I didn't reckon thar ta be a difernce."

"Sooo… let's start all over, Pete." Red slid his fingers still higher up the inside of your thigh until he could feel the hot sponginess of your ball sac and the jerk of a hefty piece of tube-steak through that thin an' much-fingered denim crotch. He squeezed your thigh one final time before removing his hand and settling back to ask, "So, tell me now; where are you from, and where are you headed? If you don't mind my asking."

Ya'd crossed your hands, put 'em in your crotch, and stretched your back 'way up as ya pushed down on your junk. With a deep sigh, ya said, "Well... I... I was born and raised down in Gray Skunk Holler. Took us 'bout a hour to git to tha Recruiter-man's office in Mama's ol' pick-up, an' then I took tha city bus from there ta here, an' now I'm on my way to Chicaga 'cause I joined the great U-nited States of America Navy this mornin'." You were bustin' out in pride all over when ya said that. Then ya went on ta add, "Goin' to a place called Great Lakes fer my Basic Trainin'. Cain't wait to git thar... wherever thar is."

"You don't say," Red replied. "That's where I'm going. I'm stationed at Great Lakes, and I've been there for almost four years, now. Just re-signed-on for a six-year hitch — and a nice bonus — and if you ever get sick or hurt or need any medical treatment, you just might be seeing me again. I'm a Corpsman, or as some of the guys prefer to call me..." he leaned over and whispered, "... a 'pecker-checker'."

"Ya mean I gotta have me a pain in my pecker afore I gits ta see ya again? Shore would be nice ta have a friend thar."

"Oh, I just bet that before the day's finished, you're gonna have lots of new friends."

"Ya think so?"

"They're gonna love ya, Pete."

CHAPTER TWO

Atennnnnnn-HUT!

And so it went. As the minute hand spun repeatedly around the clock in the airport, you and Red seemed to click into an uncanny friendship that was deeper than ya'd ever had back home on your step-daddy's tobacca farm down in Gray Skunk Holler. Almost deeper than your friendship with Darkness, but then, you really thought of him as a brother, sharin' tha same birthday an' all.

What was it that drew you to him? A friendly, helpful voice in a strange place? Or was it merely the thought of a real 'Popeye the Sailorman' in uniform? Only you could answer that question.

But at the same time that you were enjoyin' the freedom from the restrictions at home, your anxiety level was rising higher and higher. You smoked one Marlboro after another; barely a second passed after snuffing one, that you lit another.

"You always smoke like that, Petey?"

<Cough, cough>   "Naw," ya answered, "jesta bit shakey, I rucken."

"Shakey? Shakey. Ya mean nervous?"

Ya turned away, flicked some ashes into the ash can next to ya, an' kinda mumbled, "Yeah, I reckon." Ya'd heard your step-daddy's drinkin' buddies tell ya lots o' times that real men didn't never git *ner-vus*. Only the cunts and bitches got giddy 'nough to faint right away (especially when convenient to their own purposes), an' any dick-jerker who'd git *ner-vus* was a damned cock-sucker or a queer girly-man who'd scream like a guinea hen or a peacock while *she* was getting' corn-holed.

"Nothing to be nervous about, buddy. Yeah, you'll hate it at first, 'cause everything's gonna be completely new to ya, but then, by the end of the week, you'll get into the routine of Boot Camp and begin to love it. I can tell. You're gonna make a good sailor."

"Ya really thank so, Red?"

"Sure, Petey."

"Ya know, I like it when ya call me 'Petey'. Nobody's ever called me that b'fore."

◇◇◇

By the time ya finished waitin', an' that big ol' Super Constellation took off from Atlanna and then touched down in Chicago's O'Hare Airport, ya'd gone through a whole pack of Marlboro's — that's twenty cigs — in less than seven hours. Wow! Back then, ya could smoke in the airports and aboard the planes, so when ya went to get up from your seat, ya flopped back down rather suddenly, and Red had to help ya stand; you were one dizzy farm-boy, ya were.

A military bus was waiting for the new recruits, and Red told you to go on and take it up to the Training Center, "USNTC – for short," he said. He was gonna be staying in town with a… a friend… and would drive his own car, a Chevy '409', to the base the next day.

'Damn!' ya thought ta yourself. 'Jes gittin' ta know'im an' then he leaves… ta stay with somebody else tonight. Shit! Oh, well.'

There must've been every kind of guy in the world on that hour-long bus ride to USNTC, and the more you looked around, the more UN-comfortable you became. It seemed the guys were red and yellow, black, and white and brown and every shade in between, and ya knew that the preacher-man had done told ever'body that ever'body on Earth was precious in the sight of God, and that we were all brethren and sisterns... or somethin' like that. But you were only human. Some of the folks on the bus looked down-right mean and UNgodly, and you couldn't even imagine a third or fourth cousin looking that damned furry and ugly.

Ya learned later that they were from towns ya'd never heard of, around the country. Long hair down below their shoulders, short hair, or no hair at all, scruffy beards; some with one or two earrings (very unusual for men at that time) or with balls, rings, or chain-links dangling from here and there. 'Oh My God! Ouch! They got any I *cain't* see!?!'

And stink!!! My Lord! You finally figured that the odor around you came from the guy directly opposite, just across the aisle. Ya doubted that he'd had a bath in more than a month. Maybe two. Or more, butcha doubted THAT.

Eventually, after passing through a guard gate at USNTC, the bus came to a stop and forty-seven guys poured out the door at the front. Another bus was unloading at the same time, probably carrying new "troops" from the train or bus stations. Or both. Each guy — including you, Pete — was immediately swatted on the butt with what looked like a riding crop, and told to "Jump to, and stand on that mark..." painted on the tarmacadam, "... stand shoulder to shoulder, and DON'T ANY OF YOU FAGOT LADIES SAY A WORD UNTIL YOU'RE SPOKEN TO! I DON'T WANNA HEAR A FUCKIN' WHISPER OR EVEN A FART."

Once ever'one was off the busses and standin' on their marks, ya noticed a little guy about five feet six or seven inches tall, who sauntered from outta nowhere to the front of the assembled recruits. His uniform fit him so tight in all the right places, he looked like a muscle builder! He had a cute little bounce to his walk, and he had three red chevrons under a rocker on his left sleeve with four red "hash-marks" below them on his khaki uniform shirt. He was also carrying a 'ridin'-crop.'

Somewhere from the side, ya heard a thundering deep voice yell: "A-tennnnnnn-HUT!"

"Put your right hand on your neighbor's left shoulder, and then straighten out your arm," the stud with all the red decorations continued in a more civil voice. "That's how far apart you're to stay UNLESS I... AND ONLY I... TELL YOU OTHERWISE! LEARN IT FAST! I DON'T WANT TO SEE ANY OF YOU LADIES STUMBLING OVER OR TRYIN' TO FUCK EACH OTHER — unless I'm in the mood for a little sick porn... with you all spread out in front of me," he was heard to add in an almost whisper that was followed by an evil chuckle.

He continued. "ANY OF THESE OTHER UNIFORMED FUCKERS AROUND HERE GIVE YOU AN ORDER WHILE I'M WITHIN SIGHT OR EAR-SHOT, YOU WILL _**NOT**_ OBEY THEM." He glanced at the other sailors who were standing around, observing his methods. Each of them gave him the middle-finger or pumped-fist salute. Then, back to the Company he yelled, "TO YOU SHIT-HEADS, I AM GOD. I AM YOUR GOD FOR THE NEXT THREE MONTHS, AND YOU WILL... UNDER THE THREAT OF BEING BOOTED OUT OF THE NAVY... OBEY EVERY ONE OF MY COMMANDMENTS."

Pete... you, and the man up front, and most of the rest of the bedraggled wannabe-sailors jerked to a quick attention and the little guy slowly started walking back and forth, back and forth, inspecting the four rows of twenty-some raw recruits. When he came to a guy rubbernecking his every step, he stopped just off to the side of him, reached back and touched the guy's cheek with the tip of his cold, hard crop, and then gently pushed the recruit's face to the front.

Softly, almost inaudibly, he said, "Face and eyes forward, Recruit," with just the hint of a smile on his lips. Then, ever so slowly, he moved in front of the boy; the toes of their shoes touched, their knees touched, their chests touched, and yes, even the jockey-bulges in their pants touched; the poor Recruit almost fell over backwards, trying to avoid the contact. But in an instant, the eyes of the officer flared with daggers as he yelled only an inch from the trembling boy's face... "ASSHOLE!" If you saw him do it, you would've sworn he was gonna kiss the lad.

As the boy moved his hand to wipe his spray-dampened face, the man continued his momentary eardrum-splitting tirade; "DON'T WIPE MY SPIT OFF YOUR CUNT-FACE, KID. GET USED TO IT, 'cause I... or some part of me... is gonna be in your face every day for the next three months."

He went on to continue his "inspection."

Another recruit, back in the third line, was standing there, feet apart, most of his weight on one leg, cleaning the dirt from under his fingernails with a nail from his other hand, smacking and chewing gum with an open mouth, and looking around the place with total nonchalance. He looked bored-silly, and then he scratched his ass.

"You don't want to be here, do you, mister?" the hunky little man asked in a soft voice.

"Nah."

"Then why are you here?" came another gentle question.

"Parole officer said if I didn't join up, I'd go to prison."

"And why would he say that?"

"Auto theft," young guy answered as he looked to his right and then to his left, but the tip of the man's crop pulled his face forward.

"These cocksuckers are nothin' to you, and your parole officer ain't here," the man said, also looking left and right. "BUT YOU — YOU PERVERT — YOU LOOK AT ME WHEN I'M TALKING TO YOU. DO I MAKE MYSELF CLEAR?"

"Yes, Sir."

"NOW, SWALLOW IT, PUNK!"

"Sir?"

"THE GUM, YOU STUPID SHIT! I SAID, 'SWALLOW IT'."

The guy reached up with his fingers to remove the gum from his mouth.

"OH, NO, YOU DON'T, YOU DUMB CUNT! I SAID, 'SWALLOW IT'. THAT DOESN'T MEAN SPIT IT OUT AND DIRTY UP THE GROUNDS. IT DOESN'T MEAN TO STICK IT UP YOUR BUTT OR ON THE BOTTOM OF YOUR SHOE OR STICK IT BETWEEN YOUR SWEET CHEEKS AND YOUR GUMS. IT DOES, HOWEVER, MEAN TO SWALLOW THE GODDAMMED-MOTHER-FUCKIN' SON-OF-A-BITCHIN' PIECE OF SHIT YOU CALL 'CHEWING GUM'. OR MAYBE YOU'D LIKE NINE OR TEN INCHES OF MY HARD, BLACK,

COLD CROP TO PUSH IT ALL THE WAY DOWN YOUR COCK-SUCKIN' THROAT AND INTO YOUR BEER-GUT BELLY!" the man threatened, putting the thick butt-end of the crop against the kid's lips.

The sound of a quick gulp came from the poor guy's throat as the wad of chewing gum disappeared forever into the bowels of the young man who very nearly PISSED himself. "NOW STAND AT ATTENTION, DAMMITALLTOHELL!"

And so the little man continued on. "Feet together," he barked at one. "Hands at your sides," to another. "Goddammit; face and eyes FORWARD, YOU FUCKERS. HOW MANY FUCKIN' TIMES DO I HAVE TO TELL YOU DUMB-FUCK, CHICKEN-SHIT, SORRY EXCUSES OF THE HUMAN FUCKIN' RACE?" his voice rose to a screaming decibel level at yet two others.

And then, inspecting the fourth line-up, he came to YOU, Pete.

Oh, yes, you'd read everything you could find in the limited library of the little red schoolhouse in Gray Skunk Holler — everything relating to the Navy and other branches of the military. Ya knew how to *comport* yourself as a new inductee. Feet, straight ahead... not slew-footed; back, straight as an arrow; hands, sharply relaxed at your sides with your thumbs on the outside seams of your overalls, or your uniform; head, held high and facing front, as were your sparkling baby-blues.

Chicago's known as the "Windy City," and those constant winds came off Lake Michigan, across USNTC, and farther north, on into Canada. A wisp of your sun-kissed blond hair fell across your left eye but you daren't reach up and move it — not with HIM so near. But you DID scrunch up your mouth and blow your breath up and moved the hair outta your eye as you saw him approach, out of your peripheral vision.

"Well... what... do... we... have... here?" he asked ever so slowly, ever so politely, just like a true Southe'n gen'leman. Did the shirtless overalls give it away that you wuz a Southe'n boy, Petey? Huh?

"AND HE EVEN KNOWS HOW TO BLOW," he said, raising his voice above the wind so that all the new sailors could hear him. A smattering of chuckles resounded from hither, thither, and yon inflaming his ire; "YOU DICKS WEREN'T GIVEN PERMISSION TO LAUGH!" he roared to the men. Slowly, he walked completely around you, his eyes darting up and down, taking in every inch and every curve and bulge that you displayed through those too-small overalls. You couldn't see it, but when he saw those perfect glutes, he bit his lower lip and his eyes went almost shut. Then, stopping just to the side of you, with a sickeningly sweet tone he said, "Front and center, Seaman Recruit. Follow me," he ordered, turned and leisurely wove his way through the three front lines of guys standing just an arm's length from each other.

But there was no leisure with the way you followed his order, was there, Pete? No. One quick step Forward; stop. A sharp Right Face; stop. Another quick step Forward; stop. A sharp Left Face; stop. Forward through the lines until you were just to the side of the little man who had turned to face the pathetic looking collection of the rag-tag newbies. Stop. Right toes on deck behind left heel; quickly turn About Face; click heels together. "Present as ordered, Suh!" ya clearly and strongly enunciated — ya sounded like a 'Johnny Reb' — standing straight and looking forward as HE had been instructing during the past… who knew how long? Minutes? Hours? It seemed like an eternity to ya. Your throat was dry; your lips were crackled in the wind. But you were happy, at last, to be in the Navy.

"Gentlemen… and I use the term… VERY… loosely," he announced. "Here, standing before you, is the most perfect model of Seamen Recruits I have ever had the pleasure of inducting. Note the stance — the attitude — the pride at being on a military base of the United States of America, ready to be trained for the greatest good to the Service and the Country.

From the corner of your eye, you could see that he'd turned his head and was again peering at your somewhat clothed body. Up from your feet and down from your head, and back up again. He moved a bit and was soon standing right in front of you, his back to the others.

"Look me in the eyes, boy," he ordered in a barely audible tone. Your baby-blues jerked to focus on his, and you noticed that they were almost the same color as the cute little smoky-gray skunks that lived near your shack-of-a-home in the holler. You were finding it very hard to keep from smiling at the fleeting but pleasant memories of all your little Nature Friends, but you managed to succeed.

"I'm not going to hurt you, boy," he said very quietly so that no one else could hear him. "Just do what I order, and don't move unless I tell you to… or you'll live to regret it."

You started to say something but he stopped you immediately. "I said, 'Don't move,' and that includes your lips as well. There'll be a time for you to move'em, I guarantee ya, that. Now, blink your eyes once for yes or two for no. Understood?"

<Blink>

"All right. Now, don't move, and remember... I'm not going to hurt you... so long as you obey my orders." He was still speaking very softly, but just then — with the wind blowing, and with his back to the others, he yelled the order, "ARMS STRAIGHT OUT TO THE SIDES, RECRUIT."

Instantly, you obeyed. You almost looked like you were ready to be nailed to the cross. So innocent. So pure. So beautiful. And still, a slight smile on your face. So angelic.

Turning his head slightly to the others, he said, "See how quickly he obeys an order? I expect that same speed and obedience from each and every one of you until after your graduation in three months' time. That is... IF you lazy shit-asses can graduate at all!"

Without waiting for any response from the Company, he turned back to ya and WINKED! That's right... WINKED at you. Your eyes grew large as saucers, and with a light frown, he mouthed, "Don't move."

Were ya scared, Pete? You didn't know'im from Adam, if he was a good guy or a bad guy. But then... 'How could anybody with a bouncy jaunt, a cute smile, and gorgeous smoky-gray eyes be bad at all?' ya wondered.

His hands reached up and he undid the clasp of the right-shoulder strap of your overalls and tossed it over your back. You almost reacted but stopped when ya heard him issue "Shhhhh" from his lips just before he licked them moist with his pinkish-red tongue. He winked again, then undid the clasp on the left-shoulder strap. Holding it in place until he stepped completely to the left side of you, he then flicked the strap toward your backside, causing both the back bib and the front bib of the overalls to fall and begin their slide toward the deck... the tarmacadam... exposing your total nakedness. Once or twice he had to use, however slowly and sensually, the tip of his riding crop to help the denim over a bulge here, a bag of royal jewels there, or a bubbled curve back there somewhere.

"My, my, my!" he exclaimed. "Going commando, eh? Ya won't be doing that for long… regulations, ya know! But there WILL be times for that; SPECIFIC times!"

As your arm muscles flexed to help you grab the falling material, you heard him utter, "Hunh unh." So you tried to restrain any arm movement, but you DID start to inch your hands to cover your manhood.

"Hunh unnnh!" you heard again, a little louder, and made your hands return to their required place.

"Now, THIS…" he gestured with his crop from your head to your feet — without touching you — "…THIS is what I'm gonna *TRY* to mold everyone of you ladies into, within the next three months, even though I know for some of you, that'll be fuckin' impossible."

He lifted the crop once again and put the tip on your left shoulder. "Just look at these muscular arms," he said over the sounds of the wind, and the tip of the crop slid ever so gently down the length of your arm. Ya shivered in response, taking a sharp intake breath and a silent pleading prayer to your pecker to behave itself.

But prayers are not always answered the way you want them to be.

"And these pecs," came the words as the black, rubber tip then slowly inscribed an infinity symbol [∞] around your nipples, which were standing tall and firm in the chill of the afternoon's oncoming wind from the lake. Your breathing became more labored, and ya felt that all-too-familiar 'tingle in your dingle' returning. "Look at this tight six-pack," he ordered, louder still, and the crop seductively slid between the ridges of the muscles. "It'll end up being an eight-pack, by the time I get through with… 'youse guys'," he mimicked the well-known New York colloquialism.

At the stimulation, your little cock, which lay hidden in your thick bush of light blond pubic hair began to prove that you were a grower, rather than a shower. And grow, it did. And then it grew some more, not only in length but in girth as well. Not only were you to become known as one who would stand out in a crowd, you quickly earned the reputation of one who could stand out to all mankind.

Eighty-some recruits were standing in front of you. Three or four uniformed sailors were standing somewhere either side of you. Two empty busses were parked directly behind you. Ya were pretty much protected from public view. When ya realized these things, dream-like, you closed your eyes, and your hips, eased your oozing cock farther toward the guys you'd soon be marching with, running with, swimming with, showering with, sleeping with... well... not really... SLEEPIN'... with! Ya wouldn't have time for that... but... ya sure could hope; couldn't ya, Petey-boy. Ya'd moved ever-so-slightly with an unconscious, uncontrollable thrust toward the Company.

<WHACK!>

Ya'd only moved with a tiny li'l ol' thrust. And then the pain came.

Your eyes flew open and ya nearly doubled over and knew that HE had 'whumped' your leaking cock with his riding crop.

Whispering in rapid fire, he ordered, "Stand up straight, Recruit; hands to your sides; don't touch yourself." Your little monster grower had quickly retreated and hid in cover, but HE lightly nudged and lifted your balls with the length of his crop, and your dick began to grow again. Lightly rubbing the underside of your balls and the length of your cock, and then sliding the crop back and forth against your taint, your little playmate grew longer and fatter until it was drippin' upright against your belly-button.

"See how quickly he bounces back, standing tall and ready for action?" he asked the stunned Company. He permitted them a little liberty to rub, stroke, or scratch their growing, throbbing erections, their mouths agape, their eyes as big as saucers — except for those few who'd closed their eyes in disgust at the sensual beauty of male erotic nudity.

"YOU..." he yelled to each member of the Company, "... YOU are the lowest scum on the earth. There is none lower than you."

Some murmuring began to occur within ranks.

"RECRUITS... ATENNNNNNN...HUT! YOU WILL STAND AT ATTENTION UNTIL I RELEASE YOU ALL — ONE WAY OR THE OTHER — OR UNTIL YOU PASS OUT, YOU COCKSUCKERS!"

Frightened emotions became chiseled on the faces of the majority of the Company, while only a few others smiled in anticipation of being 'released' by the hunky Drill Instructor or whatever he was.

For the next several minutes, not a word was spoken. With measured step, HE slowly, deliberately, passed each man — again as if for inspection — teasingly and very lightly passing the tip of his crop across their chests as he stared into this one's eyes, and then that one's, and on and on until he had gazed menacingly into each of the eighty-eight pair in Company 209.

Well... eighty-seven pair in reality, for the eighty-eighth pair belonged to Pete, who was yet, with great diligence — considering the chill of the wind blowing in off the lake — standing there, still boned-up and blushing, facing the Company.

"THAT, Recruits, demonstrates how fast I want each of you to recover when you fall or fail to accomplish the goals I've set for you. I have four classes of recruits each year, and for the past three years, I've had MY Companies judged 'Most Outstanding' of all the Companies graduating USNTC. And I don't intend to lose that recognition! Believe me; you don't wanna know what WILL happen to your sorry asses if you make me come NEAR to losing that honor. I promise you!"

Then he turned to you, Pete, and said, "Put your clothes back on and get back in formation, Recruit."

From behind you, he watched as you bent over, exposing your nether regions as you pulled up your overalls. He even helped by tossing the straps over your shoulders again — to the front. Then, as you reversed your sharp, brisk little march back to where you had been in line-up, he announced to the Company: "My name is Chief Petty Officer David Jones. I'm your Company Commander and I'm an enlisted man just like you — NOT a commissioned officer. You will NOT call me 'Sir'. You will NOT call me 'Mister'. Those are titles of respect reserved for commissioned officers only. You will call me 'Chief Jones' or simply 'Chief', but nothing else, MEN, or you'll have hell to pay. Remember that."

"We're now going to have roll call. When you hear your name, you will take one step forward with your left foot, bring your right foot sharply to it, yell out 'Here, Chief', then step back with your left foot, and bring your right foot sharply back to it."

He started with... "Aaronson, Josiah."

<Step. Step.> "Here, Chief." <Step. Step.> Perfectly executed.

"Appleby, Curtis."

<Step. Step.> "Here, Chief." <Step. Step.> Perfectly executed again.

"Balanchine, Anthony."

<Step. Step.> "Here, Chief." <Step. Step.> Also perfectly executed.

"Beckerman... Black... Boissevain... Burnside... Calamari... Cort... Cox..."

<Step. Step.> "Here, Chief." <Step. Step.> Again and again.

'This can't be,' he thought to himself. 'No fuck-ups?' "Dix, Peter..." he called out, but as soon as his own ears heard his yelled words, he realized that it sounded like 'Dick's Peter'. Several muffled snorts and chuckles could be heard — even through the wind — and, actually blushing, he almost lost it. Without looking up from the list, he lowered his head farther and covered his face with his right hand.

<Step. Step.> "Heah, Chief." <Step. Step.>

Chief Jones recognized that voice with the Southe'n twang. He looked up and stared at the recruit for a long minute, keeping his private thoughts to himself. "Son..." he finally began, "... who in fuckin' hell gave you a name like that?"

"My mama, s... uhhh... CHIEF." It was gonna be hard for ya NOT to say "sir" like ya'd been taught was respectful ever' since ya was a boy, wasn't it gonna be, Petey?

Chief Jones removed his combination cap and scratched his head, thinking, then after a bit, replaced the cap and asked, "Do you have a middle name, Dix?"

"Yes... Chief." Nothing more was forthcoming; you had simply answered the question.

"I'm waiting."

"What for... Chief?"

A few snickers were heard.

"YOUR MIDDLE NAME, Recruit!"

"Oh! It's Balzak, Chief. That was my mama's last name afore she hadda marry my daddy."

The entire Company burst forth in raucous laughter. Even the Chief had to turn his back to them, let the laughter out, and then compose himself before calling for Attention and turning around to complete roll call.

The faces of the quickly quieted Company showed that each man was struggling to keep silent. Their jerky breathing and bouncing shoulders betrayed them even more.

"Seaman Recruit Peter Balzak Dix..." The Chief tried to begin again, but his own and the Company's unleashed and unrestrained laughter thundered across the Receiving Drill Field with the wind.

"Chief? If I may?" you were emboldened to ask, and the others immediately became silent — they wanted to hear every hilarious word you were to utter.

"Yes, Recruit; what is it, now?"

"Well, actually, Chief, my first name on my birth certificate is Peters... not Peter."

All hell then broke loose. Everyone was imagining the name, 'Peter's Ball-sacks [and] Dicks'. Recruits were guffawing, goof-offing, jumping up and down, holding their stomachs, kneeling down pounding the deck with their fists, and some were rolling on the deck in gay hilarity. No new Company at USNTC had ever begun on such a happy, fun-filled note. Surely no one would want to be '*released*' from service and miss out on anything.

The Chief just threw his hands in the air and let the roll-call list fly with the breeze. He called for order and then said, "All right, Recruits... get back on the busses. They'll take you to the barracks, your home for the next three months. Get in formation just like you are now, only alphabetically rather than random as you did this time. I'll meet you there, TRY to finish roll call, and march you over to the pecker-checker's so ya can get your dicks and ball-sacks handled… <har-har-hardy-har-har>… All pecker checkers like to handle Seamen." Chief Jones could not control himself.

Without regaining order, he called out, "I think we've had enough of Cox, Dix, and Peters for one roll-call. DISMISSED."

Then to himself, he thought, 'This is gonna be the sexiest Company I've ever fuckin' instructed. I'm gonna have my hands full. I hope.'

CHAPTER THREE

Induction & the 'Pecker-Checkers'

"I ain't got no cherry, and I ain't no cherry-picker neither," you said to one of the recruits back on the bus for the ten-minute ride over to Barracks 209, your home-away-from-home for the next ninety-or-so days. Of course, you were referring to the fruit that grows on trees and not the metaphorical 'cherries' that men give up the first time they're ever fucked down the throat or up the ass. The recruit had just said he'd bet anything that Chief Jones was gonna pluck your 'sweet cherry' before your ninety days were up.

That was enough to set off the guys seated around you, into another fit of laughter joined with cat-calls and wolf-whistles. But one guy — who you later found out went by the name of 'Slick O'Hoolihan – Ass Kicker', so-named after one of his great-grandfathers, stood up and yelled over the boisterous shenanigans: "Ya hear that, lads? Sweet-cheeks here ain't got no cherry, *and* he ain't no cherry-picker, neither. That means he likes to bottom, so whatcha say, ya horny lads?"

Well, Pete, in all your innocence, you'd never heard that expression before. You only knew that the 'bottom' was the lowest part of the pasture or field where you grew your own fodder for the few mules and jackasses and milk-cows your step-daddy had.

Like a bolt of lightning, eight or ten hands were grabbing at you. Ya didn't know how many for sure. One was covering your mouth so ya couldn't be heard yelling, and more were yanking down your shoulder straps or ripping your coveralls off. Rough, bitten fingernails carelessly tore into the flesh of your arms, pectorals, and ass-cheeks, bringing forth drops of blood. Not many, but a few.

One minute, two minutes, an eternity of time passed in only a few brief seconds, and then the bus came to a screeching halt. Everything happened so fast. The breaks squealed and the bus jerked forward and backward, sending your attackers sprawling into the aisle and across metal-barred seat backs. The handlebar swung the door open (like on school buses), and someone, somewhere was honking out an S.O.S.... beep beep beep, beeeeep beeeeep beeeeep, beep beep beep.

"What the hell's going on back there?" the driver yelled, running down the aisle to all the commotion. He was a brute of a guy himself. Probably in his late forties. Shiny, shaved head. Built like a weight-lifter. Looked strong as an ox. The chicken-shit ruffians scampered and dashed around him toward the front of the bus; one quickly dived below his crotch and between his legs to crawl away. He, the civilian driver, could have easily dropped any one or two or three, or ALL five of them, but his attention was on you!

'Oh, My God! Not him, too,' you must have thought.

It was then that you realized that your savior was black. Being a good ol' Southe'n boy, you immediately thought that the brute was gonna join the damned bigoted white-trash Yankee bullies. But what happened next was just another step in the eventual changing of the way you had been raised to think of people with skin darker than your own, except, that is, for Shadrach, Vashti, and Darkness — bless their souls — they wuz family!

"You okay, boy?" he asked, offering his hand, after breaking up the little rough-and-tumble ruckus. And then another confrontation broke out when three Shore Patrolmen scurried into the bus, grabbing the guilty-looking trouble-makers.

"Yes, suh," ya mumbled, stumbling to get up off the dirty, black rubber runner stretching down the aisle so's ta be able ta pull your pants up.

"You're bleeding, son," the driver said with some alarm just before he turned to the SPs and yelled, "Get'em out, an' hold'em. They've drawn blood."

"They's jes' li'l scratches, suh," ya said in a softer voice than his yell, getting the britches part of the coveralls pulled up over your privates. No, that's not right. 'Privates' are in the Army — over your... 'playmates.' "Ain't nothin' wrong. I've scratched m'self on rusty ol' barb-wire fencin'." The left shoulder strap was finally back in place. "Then, 'cause o' the rain, I slipped in some hog shit or mule droppin's or mushy cow-pies. Nevah caught no diseases from all tha crap; ain't gonna catch nothin' from a few li'l ol' fingernail scratches — dirty or not." As ya pulled the right shoulder strap back into place, ya said, "Ya shoulda seed what the ol' gator done to m'leg." Ya used your hands to slap both sides of your right calf. "Now, that hurt a bit, from the git-go, and we shore ain't got no proper doctorin' down in our neck o' the swomp."

"Well, if you're sure..." he began as you nodded in the affirmative, "... uhhh... what's your name, son?"

"Most folks jes call me Pete. Last name's Dix... D-I-X." Scrunchin' down to look out the windows, ya asked, "Is that Barracks 209 over yonder, suh?"

After he nodded, ya said, "I best be gettin' off the bus and gittin' in the line-up afore Chief Jones comes back. Ever'body else is already got off," ya said, trying to move around him.

"Okay, but before you go, son... Pete..." he further hesitated.

"Yes, suh? Whatcha tryin' ta say, if ya don't mind my askin'? The Chief'll be here purty soon. Jus' say it, suh."

"Pete, you don't seem upset by what nearly happened to you. From everything I saw, it looked like you came very close to being..."

You cut him off by raising both of your palms in front of him. "Please! I'm okay. Nothin' serious happened. Let's jes' let it go; okay, suh?"

"But..."

"Sir…" you interrupted him in soft but perfectly clear Standard American English, "…I might talk like an uneducated hick, but I graduated from high school…" you said with no dialect at all — down-home or otherwise. But then ya went rite back to your familiar Southe'n drawl; "…an' I did me some readin' by an English author who wrote the words for his-soon-to-be-carved marble headstone. It said:

'Life is a jest, and all things show it.
I thought it once, and now I know it.'
[John Gay: 1685-1732]

An' that means that nothin' is as it seems, an' if somethin's s'posed ta happen… it will… an' there's jes' no way ta stop it."

The driver opened his mouth to say something, but no words would come out. He just stared at you as you made your way toward the front of the bus and then went down the steps to join the rest of your Company.

Petty Officer 1st Class We'we Aelred's deep, deep voice was calling the names of the recruits who had all grouped together in no particular order, just standing around looking like a bunch of misfit jerk-offs, each with one finger up his ass and one finger up his nose. As the names were called alphabetically, the guys lined up on the appointed marks in front of the barracks.

Aelred was one of Chief Jones's three Ships' Servicemen 1st Class assistants-in-training to be Company Commanders in their own right. Aelred's strange name — strange only to the non-Native-American ear — came from the fact that he was half Hopi and half Zuni. Big-boned and full of face, he was just over six feet tall, dark brown eyes, dark brown skin with a reddish glow, and the shiniest, blackest, blue-black-like coal-colored hair any Anglo could imagine. In his khaki uniform and with his hair cut to regulation military length, you began to drool when you first set eyes on him, Pete. That 'tingle in your dingle' began again, and you unconsciously grabbed your crotch and quickly readjusted its position before removing your hand. 'A bit of dark meat never hurt anybody,' you thought to yourself — not the thoughts of a good ol' Southe'n white Christian boy, but then… you WERE different, even if you didn't perzactly [Southern blending of 'perfectly' and 'exactly'] know HOW different you were.

A passing military jeep swung into a parking space nearby, and someone stepped out from the driver's seat.

Rightly so, you were more concerned with what was happening in your immediate area, so you didn't see that it was Chief Jones who had arrived on the scene.

PO First Class Aelred hesitated for a moment at one name, then, quite UN-alphabetically, called out, "Peter… Dix." A few muffled chuckles were heard as the wind was stilled for that one solitary moment in time. He had purposefully *not* pronounced the 's' on your first name.

"Yes, suh?" you replied in full voice as the wind picked up again. You were still standing at the bottom of the steps from the bus.

"Take your mark, Recruit," he ordered and you sharply went to obey, marching toward the port side [HIS left-hand side] of the approaching Chief. The nearer you came to each other, the more likely a shoulder or foot collision seemed to be evident. Your bearing was true, and the Chief began marking his steps in time with yours — probably checking your reactions. With no more than two steps apart, you both did a 'Right Oblique' [a 45° turn to the right], step, step, 'Left Oblique' [another 45° turn but to the left], and you passed each other without touching.

Aelred was about to call the next name, but the Chief, while still marching, called out, "Seaman Recruit Dix… halt!"

Pete, you and the Chief took two more steps ending in a <stomp> with feet together, and he called out, "Abooooout Face!" Simultaneously, you both put right toe behind and to the left of left heel, sharply spun 180° to the rear and you both then brought your own feet together with another <stomp>.

"Tell me, Recruit; where did you…" he began, then broke his rigid posture, quickly stepped toward you, and asked with concern, "Is that blood on your arms and…" he unsnapped the clasp on your left shoulder strap, "… your chest?"

Before you could answer, Jones turned his head left and right looking at his assistants, yelling out, "WHAT THE FUCK HAPPENED HERE? WHY DIDN'T SOMEONE SEND DIX TO SICKBAY?" With no answer coming forth, he continued his tirade. "ALL RIGHT, YOU DWEEBS... WHICH SON-OF-A-BITCH ONE OF YOU IS GONNA ANSWER ME?"

"Sir... uhhh... Chief? If I mite?" you asked, timidly slipping back into your drawl.

He jerked his head back to look into your eyes. "WELL?... Do you have an explanation for..." his hands swung out gesturing toward several of the bloody spots, and then made swats of disgust toward his assistants, "... for all this?" Once again he gestured toward your scratches.

"Well, Chief... it's like this. The driver o' tha bus was concerned, an' I'm shore he wanted ta do that, but I refused 'cause I ben thru a lot more shi... uhhh... STUFF in my life back home. It ain't no cause uv alarm, Suh... CHIEF."

"How did it happen?" he asked.

Again, before you could answer, the civilian bus driver and a Shore Patrolman hurried over and, between the two of them alternately talking over each other, related the incident to the Chief. They also pointed out the five miscreants — handcuffed together — who were being detained by the two other SPs.

"GET'EM OVER TO THE BRIG AND HOLD'EM TILL I CAN QUESTION'EM, M'SELF," Jones ordered.

Jabbering over each other, you heard the nearby SP say, "Yes, right away, Chief," and "WHAT?" from one of the five. "YOU CAN'T DO THAT," yelled another. "THE BRIG?" asked a third, while a fourth screamed, "FOR THAT LITTLE COCKSUCKIN' FRUIT?" That one sounded like the Ass Kicker, Slick O'Hoolihan. But the fifth remained quiet and looked deflated and downtrodden.

The Chief walked toward the five and enunciated each of the individual words that followed... very clearly. "I... can... do... whatever... the fuck... I... want, mister, and... one more word outta you... and you'll... be on... your way... back to your ghettos... and parole officers... and abusive... corn-holin' fathers... and mothers... who want... nothing more... than a stiff dick... including yours... up their cum-drippin' cunts... you... mother-fuckin' sons-o'-bitches. Now shut your cocksuckin' mouths… tighten up your twitching assholes… and get the fuck outta here."

The bus took the SPs and the five troublemakers across the base to the brig where they were booked into minimum security… for the time being.

Petty Officer Aelred finished the alphabetized roll-call, discovering more *interesting* names: 'Gay, John' [a direct descendant of the John Gay who wrote his own epitaph quoted above], 'Peabody the 3rd, Floyd Alexander' [about whom, more will soon be said], 'Strait, Randy', 'Wanker, Dick' [not Richard], and 'Pisser, Hefty'.

"'Piser', sir… like 'Kiser' or 'Pfizer'," came a squeaky, timid little voice from the back as he began his jaunt to the appointed mark. Surely, if he lasted through the strenuous exercises and training, and if he could tolerate the probable harassing about his name and his weight, the chubby little guy would lose forty or fifty or even sixty pounds within the next three months.

Four abreast and at arms' length apart [left and right, front and back], the Company of eighty-eight men had been reduced to eighty-three. Chief Jones stood two arm-lengths to the left-front of the four-column formation at Recruit Aaronson's left.

"We begin a march when the leader… that's ME, or someone I appoint… when the leader calls out, 'Haaarch!' and then begins the count, 'One… Two… Three… Four', setting the time — the pace — of the procession. On the *next* count of 'One', you step forward with the left foot. Now… are there any of you mentally deficient imbeciles who do not know your left from your right?"

He waited for a response, but none was forth coming.

"All right, you fuckin' ladies, 'fess up! There's always a few of you who don't know. ALWAYS, I tell you, sooooo…" he changed his expression from that of a shit-ass commander to that of a camp-follower lass, batting his eyelids, puckering his lips, and wiggling his hips, "… sound off… NOW!" He roared the last word with an immediate physical change back into Masterly, macho masculinity.

"Here, Chief," came the timid voices of three or four recruits, among whom, he noticed, was Recruit Piser.

"Front and center, Fister!"

No one moved.

"FISTER!... Pister?... Pisser?... Piser?... PISER! FRONT AND CENTER... NOW!... HOP TO IT!"

Husky Hefty Piser did a fast, tiny-stepped but obedient walk — not a march — to stand in front of Chief Jones. His cheeks and ears glowing a beautiful shade of red. Or was it a blush? Or embarrassment?

"Present as ordered, s... uhhh... Chief," he barely was able to say aloud.

"Extend your left hand, Recruit."

He quickly obeyed, arm straight out, fingers together, palm down. Several muffled chuckles were heard from the Company. He frowned.

"Good form, Recruit, but wrong arm and hand." Down went the wrong right hand, and up came the right left hand. "Verrry googoood," Jones said in an insulting manner. "Now for you and a few of your... eighty-two bunkmates..." he wriggled his eyebrows at Piser and looked out across the Company, "...a bit of information for you to learn." In a cracking, untrained voice, he sorta sang a sing-song mimic of the Army's cadence, "'You're in the Navy now'... and, IF any of you Recruits make it out of Boot Camp, most of you will likely be given orders for sea duty... on ships — AND DON'T EVER REFER TO THEM AS BOATS! We'll get to that later, in one of your classes. But back to what I was about to say. Ships have two LONG sides — the right side and the left side, as you face forward. The right side is called the Starboard, and the left side is called the Port. The word 'left' has four letters in it; the word 'Port' has four letters in it; left and Port are the same! Simple? Yes? No?"

Piser was slightly nodding his head, which was tilted to the left, but a frown was on his brow, and his eyes were cast toward the deck.

"Okay, I can see that some of you are still having a little problem," the Chief said. He let out a deep, disgusted sigh and threw his head back, with eyes closed. His hands — dramatically together — he brought up under his chin as if he were saying his prayers, like a good little boy, to the one un-named God, or to Neptune, or to Mercury, the god of learning. A moment later and after another deep sigh, with head, eyes, and hands as usual, he began the lesson once more.

"ALL RECRUITS..." he called out, "...some of you are wearing wedding bands; some of you HOPE to be wearing wedding bands at some future date; and some of you fuckers are afraid that if you WERE to wear a wedding band, you'd lose the chance of getting another sweet piece of dripping pussy or tight ass. Did THAT get your attention, you cocksuckin', pussy-lickin' boys? Okay, I want everyone to raise your arm with the hand that either DOES, or WILL HAVE, or SHOULD BE the hand with the finger that a wedding band would be placed on."

Surprisingly, it appeared that everyone knew the correct hand. He went on to add, "Like 'Port', 'band' and 'ring' also have only four letters — the same as 'left'. From this point on, I want you to remember this four-letter word. It ain't twat, or hell, or piss, shit, damn, fuck, suck, pork, fist, or the CUNT that most of you will HAVE in every <u>PORT</u>! CUNT... FOUR LETTERS! PORT... FOUR LETTERS! LEFT... FOUR LETTERS! DON'T FORGET IT!!!"

At the recitation of all those nasty, nasty words, you and everyone else of the other recruits were showing the effects of Omar the tent-maker in your trousers. Well... almost everyone else.

Raised eyebrows, faint smiles, a nod here, a nod there, several close-eyed thrusts, showed Jones that once again he had given a lesson, no matter how small, with which his men had connected.

"As you were, Recruit," he said to Piser, gesturing toward the mark that had been vacated.

When Piser was back in formation, Jones yelled out, "You fuck-ups saw Recruit Dix do it correctly the first time it was ordered. Let's see just how observant you were."

Four rows of twenty or twenty-one new recruits were facing Chief Jones. He called out, "Riiiiight FACE!"

'Ohhh, the pain of it all,' he thought to himself, left arm crossing his chest, right elbow on left hand, and forehead being supported by right hand. He had been correct in calling them 'fuck-ups,' for nearly everyone floundered with the execution of the command, even *with* the lesson on left and right.

"Ya wanna send'em all home with Mental Deficiency Discharges, Chief?" yelled one of his assistants-in-training.

Jones slooowly let his piercing smoky-gray eyes peruse each and every one of the recruits in formation. He didn't care how fuckin' long he took, nor how long he made them stand at Attention. They could stand like that through chow time, or even bunk time for all he cared, till each and every one of them collapsed from thirst, from hunger, or from sleeplessness. But he knew he couldn't do that to them. Finally, after several long minutes, he looked back at his assistants and replied, "No, but we're gonna have to work our asses off to get these retards shaped up enough just to get'em out of Great Lakes. Every damned Company's getting worse than the last one."

Then, sounding a bit like some irritated future Captain James T. Kirk, he ordered, "Company, Face… *thataway!*" he said, pointing with his shiny, black riding crop while executing a sharp Left Face, so that he and they would all be facing the same direction.

And then he began.

> *"Haaarch!*
> *One… two… three… four, gimme your*
> *left, right, left, gimme your*
> *left, right, left, gimme your*
> *Hup, two, three, four*
> *Hup, two, three, four."*

Then he began a singsong marching cadence:

> *"There WAS a YELLow BIRD*
> *WITH a YELLow BILL*
> *That LANded ON my WINdowSILL.*
> *I GOT it IN with a PIECE of BREAD*
> *And SMASHED its LITtle HEAD.*
> *WELL, the MOral IS:*
> *If YOU want HEAD, ya NEED the BREAD.*
> *There WAS a YELLow Bird…"*
> etc., etc., etc.

Over and over, again and again, little by little, nearly every member of the Company learned the words to the cadence. Then, after four more "Hup, two, three, fours," he began another marching cadence:

> *"Everywhere we go*
> *people want to know*
> *who we are*
> *so we tell them...*
> *We ain't the Air Force*
> *playin' on the golf course*
> *We ain't the Army*
> *the backpackin' Army*
> *We ain't the Marines*
> *they don't even look mean*
> *We are the Navy*
> *the world's finest Navy*
> *the mighty, mighty Navy.*
> *Everywhere we go..."*
> etc., etc., etc.

After several rounds of that one, the marching was looking somewhat better, and the recruits were more in step than earlier. The motley assemblage of males had marched for a little more than a mile and had reached the Induction Compound.

"Companyyyyy... HALT!" Jones ordered. At the moment, they were in four columns of twenty or twenty-one men each. "If you had a couple months' training under your belts — you numb-skulls would need that long — I'd give you a command that I would expect you to execute flawlessly, but..." he paused, shaking his head, then went on, "...there's not a one of you lug-heads who could possibly execute it now."

Immediately, though, he glanced at you, Recruit Dix, who had a shit-eating grin on your face. Jones raised his eyebrows and tapped his own forehead three times, silently as if you knew what he wanted to ask.

Your smile grew a little larger, and you gave a single, small nod in response.

Surprised, Jones's eyes grew larger, asking the unspoken question again.

You looked straight ahead, Pete, then nodded once to the deck, and then looked straight ahead again; your action had been a HUGE nod in the affirmative.

The Chief shook his head in smiling disbelief, and *your* darting eyes had seen it, even without moving your head. You knew that a connection had been made, deeper than was common between Commander and Recruit.

Jones moved up the four or five steps leading to the entrance of the USNTC Hospital, turned, and said, "You are now in four-column formation. I want you in one-column, single file formation. Stand at ease, talk with each other, and you have no more than five minutes to alphabetize yourselves. Any of you feel like giving me a hundred push-ups right now?"

"Sir, no Sir," came a few gung-ho, unthinking responses, which were immediately followed by several more, and then many more.

"Then you'd better be in perfect alphabetical order, Recruits. Perfect order. That's what I want! Now... forget the lead in your cocks, and get busy. You have exactly five minutes from..." He looked at his stopwatch. "...NOW!" <Click>

Tick-tock. Tick-tock.

The second hands swept around the clocks and watches.

One minute.

And a half.

Two minutes. Everyone was in place.

You decided to risk it, didn't you, Pete? You took the initiative, stepped out, and ran to the head of the single-line formation. "What's your last name, the first two letters?"

"Aaronson... A-a."

"Balanchine... B-a."

"Beckerman... B-e."

"Black... B-l."

"Burnside… B-u."

Everyone could see what you were doing. Back toward the end of the line-up, they were checking for themselves to make sure they were in the correct order.

"NO LAS' NAME. FURS' TWO LETTAHS, ONLY. SAVE TIME."

"B-o."

"You and B-u… switch." You pointed to the next guy.

"C-o."

"C-o… r."

You pointed to the guy before "C-o-r."

"C-o-x."

"Change places with each other." You pointed to the next one.

"C-a."

"Woah! Go back — what is it — two?" You pointed to the two you kinda remembered it to be.

"C-o-r," said one; "B-o," said the other.

"C-a… get between those two."

"D-i-c. 'Dickens'," he said, knowing that your name was 'D-i-x'.

"E-v."

"Save a place fer me righchere," you pointed between them. "An' thank ya, muchly."

On and on it went, Pete. Eighty-two sailors and yourself.

"U-n."

"W-i."

"Y-o."

"Zzyzx… Z-z."

It was wonderful how you got everyone in order. Most already were, but a few were out by only one or two places. Finishing, you raced back to between D-i-c and E-v, and stood there at Attention.

<Click> went the stopwatch.

"VERY GOOD, SEAMAN RECRUIT DIX," Chief Jones said loud enough for the entire Company to hear. "Five minutes, thirteen seconds. Not perfect, but damned good, I must say! You saved a few asses out there today, Dix. I saw what you did, and the Company should be proud of you."

He then raised his voice louder yet. "AND IT WAS HIS UNASKED-FOR INITIATIVE THAT SAVED YOUR LAZY ASSES. YOU KNOW WHO I'M TALKING ABOUT. NOW, IS THERE ANYONE OF YOU WHO'LL SAVE HIS ASS SOME DAY? MAYBE WHEN YOU'RE TRAINING TO BE A FIRE FIGHTER? MAYBE WHEN YOU'RE DOING MOCKUP WARFARE, USING LIVE AMMUNITION, CRAWLING ON YOUR BELLIES? MAYBE WHEN YOU'RE PRACTICING DIVING OUT OF AN AIRCRAFT, AND YOU NOTICE THAT HIS CHUTE ISN'T OPENING? WILL YOU DIVE-BOMB TO HIM, GRAB HIM, AND SAVE HIM FROM A BLOODY, BONE-SHATTERING, BRAIN-SCATTERING DEATH? WHEN HIS SUBMARINE HAS BEEN TORPEDOED AND IS SITTING ON THE BOTTOM, WILL YOU DO EVERYTHING IN YOUR POWER TO SAVE HIM AND HIS FELLOW SUBMARINERS? AND WHEN YOU FINALLY GET INTO THE BARRACKS TONIGHT, WILL YOU SHAKE HIS HAND, GIVE HIM A MANLY, FULL-BODY HUG AND A GOOD SLAP ON HIS ASS…? ALL, WHILE YOU'RE BOTH BARE-ASSED NAKED, GETTING READY FOR A SHOWER, AND THINK NOTHING OF THE FLESH TO FLESH CONTACT?" He looked straight at you, Pete, and said — with the cutest grin on a face a man ever did see — "Eighty-two slaps on your ass is your punishment for being thirteen seconds late, Recruit Dix, Peters Balzak." He chuckled and shook his head. "We gotta do *somethin'* about that name o' yours." And he winked yet again.

The Company was quiet and no one responded to Jones's questions and challenges. Not a sound was heard except for the eternal howling of the wind, and the roars of a motorcycle or Jeep passing by. Jones was devastated. He thought for a moment and then realized as he spoke without thinking…

"I HAVEN'T CALLED YOU BACK TO ATTENTION. YOU'RE STILL FREE TO LAUGH, TALK, MAKE COMMENTS, JUMP UP AND DOWN, HOOP AND HOLLER,... WHATEVER... BUT... DON'T... GET... OUT... OF... LINE, YOU FUCKERS!

Damn! He could change from friend to fuckin' sadist fiend in an instant. What hell could he conjure up during training? The possibilities were just too incalculable to begin imagining.

All hell broke loose... IN LINE. "TEAM. TEAM. TEAM. TEAM. TEAM." At the moment, it was more High School than Military enthusiasm, but it came from each man's gut. And Jones knew it in his own. The cry grew louder and louder as more and more of the recruits joined in.

"We're ONE!" "A UNIT!" "TOGETHER!" "FAMILY!" "COMPANY 209!" Individuals then yelled out in the spirit of Brotherhood.

Jones was going to be proud of them. He knew that for damn tootin'!

◇◇◇

First stop of the single-column regiment was the Barber Shop. It only took ninety seconds — a mere minute and a half for each of you to become a skinhead. With six barbers, that's less than thirty minutes your Company spent in the shop, and that's considering hop-up- and hop-down-from-the-chair time.

Next was 'Dracula's Tomb' where everyone stripped naked, stowed the clothes in lockers, and had blood, urine, and fecal samples taken for examination and testing. There was lots of scrotal squeezing, probing, coughing, and the dreaded middle-finger treatment — well... dreaded by most, anyway. And a general head-to-toe physical exam was administered and Small Pox, Polio Immunization, and several other vaccines were injected into upper arms, shoulders, butt-cheeks, and thighs. Ears and noses were poked with swabs. The insides of cheeks and the tops of tongues were fucked by more swabs, longer swabs. Eyes were checked and charts were read. Teeth and gums were probed with what felt like mining tools. Those with foreskins were told to "Skin 'em back!" More swabs collected seminal deposits."

"Why are ya doing that?" you heard Dickens, the Recruit in front of you, ask.

"Your Company'll be having Grilled Cheese sandwiches for chow tonight," the 'pecker-checker' answered, with a smart-alecky grin on his face.

You thought Dickens was gonna puke at the mention of that, but he didn't.

The circumcised guys were no luckier than you who had retained your skins, though. A sterile cotton-ended probe went about an inch-and-a-half inside every penis through the pee slit, and it burned like living Hell; it hurt so fuckin' bad, you thought you'd never take another piss as long as you lived.

And finally, you were tested for flat-footedness or not, and most of those guys who *did* have flat-feet, were very close to being medically discharged. Oh, you hoped and prayed to whatever gods or whoever that you didn't have flat-feet. You could sit at a desk and rattle paper all day long if you had to; that's how badly you wanted a career in the U-nited States of America Navy.

The 'pecker-checkers' had had absolutely no T.L.C. ['Tender Lovin' Care.'] They'd seemed bored in their jobs — one pecker, two peckers, three peckers, four; fat pecker, skinny pecker, curved pecker, 'n' more. The shots hurt like Hell, and you were hammered, jabbed, poked, prodded, and punctured to the point that when your penis was manhandled, you didn't even get an erection — you realized that you were just a briny piece of squid to them. Although… there were a couple there that… oh, what the fuck! You were in the Navy — finally. You couldn't be thinking of things like that.

After being totally humiliated — still naked — you and the others were marched single-file down to the Olympic size pool in the basement of the hospital.

Jones and his wannabes were already there and ordered the eighty-three of you to remain in single-file but, rather than at arm's length apart, they then wanted you 'cock-to-ass' with your hands at your sides and not covering your family jewels when in contact with a warm crack.

Faces turned red, ears became inflamed, fingers twitched, pits perspired, and several recruits unconsciously humped the ass-cheeks in front of them; nipples hardened and stood out like miniature penises while further 'south', the real things slowly, maddeningly, grew toward the warm, sweaty naked crevice in front of 'em, or at least to their maximum length and girth. Angered physical re-BUTT-als occurred with the rear-swat of a hand, or a head jerked back with a hateful glare or some verbal rebuke.

The guys at the front of the line had it better than those farther back — the flesh-to-flesh contact didn't last so long — and as the first six men stepped to the edge of the pool coping, it was noted whether or not an erection or stiffy merited the promise of psychological and religious examinations as well. Didn't *anyone* in authority realize that flesh is flesh and that a dick has no conscience when in the presence of a warm, sweaty, or perfumed hole, be it a fragrance made from whale vomit [ambergris], or the idea of a hole to penetrate, or a cleft to slide around in? Why feel bad about it? Enjoy the contact.

When it was your time to approach poolside, Pete, your grower of a 'rudder' was sure to slow your speed from one end of the pool to the other. There was just no way that you were going to get it to go back into hiding until you dived into the cool water.

Having difficulty coordinating breathing while doing the breaststroke, you took a VERY deep breath, dived in, and swam the entire length of the pool... underwater. Nobody back in the holler could match — much less beat — your underwater-distance abilities, and you knew it. And perhaps that little feat might get you into Navy Seals training! You hoped.

Or, looking back at those days, Pete... at least you might have had time and circumstance to acquire greater deep-throating talents and other submerged skills you'd only dreamed of. Hee hee hee.

Then you all got dressed in your 'civies', marched to the chow hall and were taught HOW to get your trays of food from the serving line.

<Splat.> <Splat.> <Splatter.> "Oops," came from the K.P. [Kitchen Police] server. No one served himself; the Navy decided WHAT and HOW MUCH you were to eat. If you didn't like what was thrown on your tray... tough shit! You'd lose your excess weight faster. And there were no seconds of anything. Not even S.O.S. 'Shit On a Shingle.' A

delicious military staple. You still eat it to this day, don'tcha, Pete? Mighty fine eatin'.

You had to stand at a table until the entire Company was standing around their own tables at Attention. You all sat as one: back straight, feet flat on the floor, left hand in lap ["NOT scratching your balls," HE'd commanded]; everyone raised his fork in unison; everyone ate in unison, chewing each bite twenty-one times; everyone drank in unison after seven bites of food; and when finished with the meal, one's right hand joined one's left on the crotch of one's *own* trousers.

It was worse than what you'd read about the dining room *étiquette* in the military academies, wasn't it, Pete? But you knew that the strictest discipline only lasted during Boot Camp. At least that's what you'd heard, and that's what you hoped for.

More marching filled the afternoon's agenda, taking you and the Company in, around, through and, in a few instances... over... the Recruit Training area of the base to familiarize yourselves with where the different buildings were located. The commissary; the post office; the public phones; the laundry; the Storekeeper (same as the Army's 'Quartermaster'); the Protestant, Catholic, and Jewish chapels; the Base Hospital; the several Sick Bays (clinics); and most important of all — the pay-master's office for your measly bi-monthly stipend. Around five o'clock... or '1700 hours' as it was referred to in military jargon, Jones finally began the final march of the day... the one back to the chow hall for supper, and then to the barracks and BED!

That first night in the barracks, 'Jones's henchmen' [his assistants-in-training] split the Company into groups of ± twenty-some-odd recruits, and taught you how to dress your bunks, so neatly and so tightly, that you could actually bounce a quarter on the blanket. And all eighty-three of you had to pass Chief Petty Officer Jones's Bunk Inspection before a single one of you could shit, shower, shave, shampoo, and hit the rack for the evening.

In your locker, each of you found a pillowcase, a bath towel, a washcloth, a can of shaving lather, and two disposable razors. The Recruiting Office had told you what NOT to bring with you, and after the Storekeeper would outfit you the next day, everything you'd worn or brought with you would either be thrown away or shipped back home. EVERYTHING! Except for glasses and wristwatches. Wallets were 'iffy', depending on their size. Dentures and partials were also 'iffy'; you might be going home with them, yourself, or they might be replaced with regulation prostheses. Butt plugs, cock rings, ball stretchers/separators, and other sex toys were not allowed at all! Rubbers (the ones for your cocks) would not ordinarily — the magic word — be necessary for the next six weeks, and therefore not allowed on your person until your first 'liberty'. The rubbers to keep your little footsies from getting wet, would be provided — when thought necessary — by the United States Navy.

After Jones had dismissed his henchmen for the evening, he called you all to stand at Attention at the foot of your bunks, *with* your bunkmate. If you had taken a top bunk, the recruit who had taken the bottom one was your bunkmate, and vice versa. Next, he ordered, "At ease, men, and introduce yourself to your bunkmate and to the bunkmates to your right and your left… AND BE QUICK ABOUT IT!"

Then he told you to strip out of your clothes… "ALL OF THEM. FOLD THEM NEATLY AND STOW THEM IN YOUR LOCKER. SOFT OR HARD, I WANNA SEE NOTHING BUT NAKED FLESH AND WHATEVER HAIR YOU HAVE… FOR RIGHT NOW."

A low grumbling began, and then grew louder. Soon you heard, "NO ARGUING. DO IT!"

CHAPTER FOUR

Getting to know you – with lather and razors

With great hesitation from nearly all, Chief Petty Officer Jones's command was obeyed. Eighty-three bodies with curly, kinky, straight body-fur, or none at all, which was not uncommon for the Native Americans, appeared two-by-two at the feet of the bunks, hands covering genitals as best they could. From Alpha Bravo Charlie to X-Ray Yankee Zulu heritage, and everything in between, could be seen: light meat, dark meat, phallocampsis [1] of every kind — major or minor, curved up, down, left, or right, or pointing out like an arrow, straight and strong; fat, skinny, short, long, or average; cut or uncut — each unique and individual in every way. Helmet, knob, bell end, mushroom, bullet shaped glans, and more. Fuck! Who really gives a good crap about all that, anyway? It ain't 'how much', but 'HOW!' that's important. Only in the porn industry is size important, and as you and I and everyone else knows, Pete, movies are an illusion of grandeur, bigger than life. Sorry to burst your bubble, but at least it's not your ass.

As Company Commander, the Chief's words had been coming from the Public Address speakers inside the dorm-like barracks since his assistants had left for the evening. The door to his private quarters was in the middle of the back wall. A large solid sheet of glass provided a window on either side of the door, and Venetian Blinds behind the windows provided privacy whenever he wanted or needed it; for all intents and purposes, they had been closed ever since your Company, Pete, had taken up residence in the barracks.

The door opened, and out stepped the studliest man in the building... not tall, but not short either... muscular, but not muscle-bound... heavy looking, but not an ounce of fat on him... his bulky but relaxed arms swung as if in parade-mode, while his body bounced up and down with each spring-like motion on the balls of his bare feet. From around his neck hung a bath towel, covering his nipples and pectorals; no other fabric hid any of his otherwise nude body. From between the tops of his hard, firm-looking thighs dangled considerably more than a handful of his surgically mutilated family jewels, neither overly blest nor regrettably cheated by Nature. Average, he was, in every way but for his attitude; he was in command because he had earned the right, and he was also in control because he was sure of himself, and he loved and cared for every one of his subordinates and underlings. He knew that he could and would forge the 'fires of transmutation' and make each and every one of his subjects the best fucking sailor the country had ever known. But then, all sailors are known for their 'FUCKING' prowess, aren't they, Pete? A girl in every port; right? But not for you, though. Oh, no! Not for you.

You were of a different stroke, alignment, persuasion, orientation, or however you chose to consider yourself; weren't you, country boy? One day — or was it more than once? — I heard you think to yourself, "I'm not any more different than anyone else is; I'm just me." And that was beautiful.

Looking more carefully — and undoubtedly more stimulating — there was something else that you noticed. Not a hair was on his chest or back. Not a hair was around his cock and balls, nor peeking out from his ass-crack. He was completely denuded from below his neck to his wrists and to the tops of his toes. A few wolf whistles and catcalls were heard in response. There was not even a 'treasure trail' leading to the jewels of the kingdom, so to speak.

"That must mean you like what you see," he kidded his men as he shook his hips. His flaccid cock slapped the hairless flesh, first to the right, then to the left, back and forth, again and again. Suddenly, the barracks went as silent as a funerary mausoleum, except for the <slap> <slap> <slap> of his oozing, fleshy tube. Several other hands covered the thickening and lengthening of other dicks while the Chief's phallus pendulously returned to its former position, albeit somewhat larger, somewhat longer, and a little more stand-outish than it had been.

"Pete... front and center... on the double!" he called out, and the only 'Peter' in Company 209 double-timed it to only a couple feet in front of the Chief. Pete's hands covered his own privates; his bare ass-cheeks and somewhat hairy ass-crack reflected glimmers of the overhead lighting to the rest of the Company.

"They've already seen you naked, Pete. Return your hands to your sides." It was done. "Abooout face!" he ordered and was obeyed. Then Jones stepped diagonally forward to stand next to you. "Stand at ease, Recruits... that means you, too, Pete... but do not cover your nakedness with your hands or towel or any other thing. Look around you; no two of us men are exactly alike. In our nakedness, we are united in our diversity. We are brothers and will be working for the common good."

By saying that, he had just won the respect and comradeship of at least ninety per cent of the Company... not counting the five bastards in the brig.

With a wiggle of his index finger and a directional nod of his head toward the showers, Jones spoke to the Company. "One of the first things I have each of my Companies do is a complete body shave, as I have now, arms, legs, back, chest, pubic area, and ass. No more 'treasure trail;' no more triangle over 'Little Junior'."

As rumblings of contempt and words of anger began and grew louder, so did Jones's voice. "Atennnnnnn-HUT!" he called, and all became quiet once more. He continued. "You're no different than all my other Companies. You're all squabblers over the little things. Little boys throwing temper tantrums at not having things the way you want them. I've the right to walk past you and slap the wrist of each and every one of you. There's no use to holler and yell and scream and bitch at what I tell you to do. I'll always win. I always have. I always will. That's why I'm a Company Commander and you're all Seamen Recruit Trainees, and if you're thinking about going over my head, I wouldn't advise it. A full-body shave below the neck is part of a new program we're instigating, and Admiral Ivey L. Sutton, Commandant of USNTC, has given full approval to pioneer this endeavor.

"And besides that, men…" he said for the first time, dropping the 'Company Commander' persona but for only a few moments, "…I want you to know that I'll never ask you to do anything that I wouldn't do, myself. More often than not, you'll find that I'm right there beside you, carrying out the order, myself, which I've just given you. Are you with me, men?"

"Sir, yes, sir," and "Yes, Chief, yes," were the mixed responses coming from nearly every one of the Recruits.

"Now, if any of you don't want to conform to the new regulation, Courts-martial can be arranged, and within a week, you'll be on your way home. Now then, by show of hands, how many of you want to GO HOME rather than have… AND KEEP… a full-body shave provided by your bunkmate, until graduation in three months? No doubt some of you have brought an army of crabs — body lice — into my Company, and I don't want that; I'll not *have* that; your hair WILL grow back *IF* you want it to, but I'll only allow it after your new orders come through. Who knows? You may find after three months that you like your smoooooth skin and sexy new look. Women shave their legs and pits and pussies for you; why don't you return the favor? Ya know… do for others as you would have them do for you. Right now, I'm the 'other'; and you'll be doin' it 'cause I'm giving the orders around here. Don't go thinking that only queers and faggots shave their cocks and balls and everything else; many athletes shave full-body, too — runners, bikers, swimmers, weight lifters, wrestlers, gymnasts… just to name a few. And if *something* should just *happen* to come up… well… nothing wrong with giving a buddy a hand, is there? You'd just be helping a neighbor out. And turn-about is fair play. He'll give you a helping hand, too. Remember the circle jerks you had when you were full of spit and vinegar and just coming into manhood? Fun, wasn't it? Well, I'm not asking you to suck somebody's cock, or to bend over to pick up the soap in the showers. Hell! Until regulations are changed — and they WILL be changed *someday* — you could get your ass kicked out of the military for doing those two things. I'm just saying there's nothing queer or faggoty about giving or receiving a full-body shave. I know my lady likes it better since I started shaving, and we've got five little rug-rats — a set of twin girls and a set of triplet boys — underfoot to prove it. And she and I have more fun now that we're shaving each other. It's part of the fun of 'togetherness'. And it's made our marriage stronger," he said, not revealing anything else about his 'holy union'.

He smiled and his dick bobbed up and down a couple of times. "So? How many of you want to leave?"

No one answered. No one raised a hand, but a lot of stud-meat had begun to stand tall.

"Thank you. I knew you'd see it my way, Recruits. Now, stand easy, but keep your hands to your sides as you follow Pete and me to the showers. I'm going to demonstrate how to shave another guy from neck to toes... and every li'l ol' inch in between. And then... THEN... it'll be your turn to DO your bunkmate. Interpret that any way you will... this ONE time."

"Awww fuck!" came a few comments.

"Ouch!" came another.

"Must I, Chief?" whined yet another.

"What's your name, Recruit?"

"Seaman Recruit Floyd Reginald Alexander Peabody the Third... Chief."

Well, let me tell you, Pete... if the name 'Peters Balzak Dix' had caused a stir, the name 'Floyd Reginald Alexander Peabody the Third' brought out an instant wave of loud and raucous ridiculing mockery of his Bostonian 'upper crust' attitude and accent. But the scene wasn't finished yet.

"Well, shit, Seaman Recruit Floyd Reginald Alexander Pea-body. An entire fucking war could be fought and won in the time it takes to call out your fucking name." Jones began but stopped upon being, THANKFULLY, interrupted. If he'd tried to continue, he'd have broken into uncontrollable laughter at *attempting* a stoic appearance. The Company, however, had absolutely no compunction in letting loose with an uncontrollable roar of laughter at what they'd just heard.

Nevertheless, Recruit Peabody courageously strove to continue forthwith. "Do forgive the interruption, Chief, but if I may be permitted to correct the Chief's enunciation of the Recruit's family name?" he politely asked, to which Chief Jones gave an expressionless but intrigued and respectful nod. A sudden hush ensconced the dormit'ry of the barracks.

"The proper elocution and intonation of the phonetics is (pē'-bəd-ē); not (pē-**bäd'**-ē), and not (pē-**bud'**-ē)... Chief."

Need there be mentioned the renewed outbreak of boisterous gaiety and thunderous hilarity created by and directed toward the obviously spoiled, babied, and catered-to, poor little rich brat? He seemed not to be affected one iota by the cantankerous, bawdry responses of those ignorant, bestial paddywhackers 'beneath' his rightful place in the society of milit'ry ranks. He stood tall in his self-assurance, while his own family jewels — modest but adequate in their longitudes and latitudes for, firstly, propagating the family name and, secondly, for *some* degree of personal enjoyment — hung deliciously flaccid, lacking any masculine vigor whatsoever.

Chief Jones had seen his kind before — arrogant and full of self-importance and esteem, <u>probably</u> knowing that his daddy, <u>probably</u> a Senator from the proud Colony/State of Massachusetts, <u>probably</u> would be able to "fix it all" at any seemingly appropriate time or circumstance. Jones would find out soon enough, when he had time to peruse each recruit's induction file. But for the time being, he had another... more devious... question in mind.

"Recruit... (pē'-bəd-ē)..." he very carefully emphasized the 'phonetically correct' family name.

"Yes, Chief?"

"Who is your bunkmate?" he asked, looking around.

With eyebrows and chin raised, he proudly answered, "I chose an upper bunk, Chief, though I've been led to believe that the correct term for same is 'rack', and Recruit Peters Dix chose the lower one. Therefore, obviously, I am above him, as he is below me, and I..."

Pete... I swear, you jerked your head toward... oh, how shall we call him?... and glared at him for his asinine insinuation. Though he was somewhat larger than you, you knew that he wouldn't stand a chance in hell of beating you at wrastlin' in a puddle of pig shit or cow paddies down in Okefenok. But before you could say or do anything else, good ol' Chief won the moment.

"Recruit (pē'-bəd-ē)..." he interrupted the prideful diatribe.

"Yes, Chief?"

"Well, at least I see you're quick to respond," he changed his line of thought for the moment.

"Oh, yes, Chief. I'll always be the first to respond. You'll recognize that meritorious behavior soon enough." A snide smile crept across his face as he 'patted himself on his back', so to speak.

A group of deep-throated… errr… deep-TONED cynical 'Ooooo's' and 'Ahhhh's' came from the Company, anxious to see how the little smart-ass and the Masterful Big-ass were going to rumble. Jones glared around in silent rebuke at the offenders, then kindly looked back to… awww, shit! Let's everybody just call him… 'Alex'. It's easier than relating the tale with phonetic letters.

"Are you sure," Jones asked, "that you'd prefer the upper bunk?"

"Oh, yes, Chief. That is… unless *you'd* prefer otherwise."

What a fuckin' suck-up! He cocked his head to one side, genteelly nodded in obeisance to his superior, raised his eyebrows questioningly, and his devilish smile returned.

"You can sleep in the shit-house for all I care, ALEX, though I can clearly guesstimate that you're referred to by the appellation 'Alex-ZHAHN-der' back home." That brought about a goodly number of restrained chuckles from the rest of the Company. "But, be that as it may, you might end up doing just that — sleeping in the shit-house, I mean — some night after the Company's marched and hiked twenty or thirty miles, non-stop and double-time, and you're finally sittin' on the crapper before hittin' the rack. But instead, you fall dead asleep, slip off the seat without wiping yourself, and land straddling the bottom of the commode with your… spread-eagled… legs, and with your cheek and nose lying in a putrid puddle of piss. Oh… and perhaps with one of your own turds slowly inching it's juicy way out of your shitty ass."

"Right on, Chief." "Way ta go." "Anyone gotta Polaroid? Sure wish they were on the public market right now!" "When do we march?" came repugnant responses from the rowdy recruits.

"I was just thinking, ALEX..." Jones continued, "...we eat a lot of cabbage in the Navy — cabbage rolls, stuffed cabbage, corned beef and cabbage, cabbage soup, sauerkraut, coleslaw — for the roughage and all that, ya know. And cabbage builds up a lot of gas in the intestines. And that is the WORST smelling gas any human body can manufacture." He looked out over the Company and said, "We should bottle or canister it and use it for all our Navy vehicles."

All kinds of comments and guffaws came from that remark, and then he returned his attention to Alex. "Now, if you're on top and Pete's on bottom... of the bunks... racks, I'm talking about... and he's had cabbage for supper... and *if* he can't help but expel a nice, long, warm, juicy fart, then you, Alex, are going to be the recipient of the fumes of the afterburner as the warm gas rises from the bottom... *rack*... to the upper."

Jones looked over to you, Pete, and winked with a grin once again. You winked back at him and returned the grin... forgetting that twenty or thirty, or maybe forty of the recruits could easily see the exchange.

"Are you quite sure you want the top bunk, Recruit?"

"Well, Chief, it is rather small up there, and I do tend to toss and turn when in the arms of Morpheus..." his then serene smile indicated that he felt confident he'd just demonstrated his superior intelligence before all. Soon, he would become RCPO [Recruit Chief Petty Officer] or, at the very least, RLPO [Recruit Leader Petty Officer]. He just *KNEW* it for a certainty.

"Ohhh, brother!" came an exclamation from somewhere.

"Arms of Morpheus, eh? How many wet dreams does *HE* give you each night... Alex, baby?" shouted one of the guys in the back.

"Does Morpheus' naked, youthful daddy, Hypnos, ever awaken, put his legs together, and rise from his coverless divan or squab?" asked another.

"That'll be enough of that, BOYS!" Jones shouted back. Muted laughter followed throughout the room. Even from the Chief, himself.

That last suggestive question had shaken Alex to the core, discovering that someone else in the Company had as much knowledge of mythology as he. If not more. But he'd have to expand on his areas of pure brilliance. Yes; back home — out on Margaret's Vineyard — Mummy and Daddy would use that word, 'brilliance', wouldn't they? Yes, of course. And it would be ever so nice to commodore the helm of Daddy's yacht, which was named 'The Tethys and Thetis'. Yes, ever so nice.

Alex was yanked back into the naked present when at last he heard Chief Jones calling, "Alex… Alex… Seaman Recruit FLOYD REGINALD ALEXANDER PEABODY THE THIRD!"

"Sir? Oh! Yes, sir, Chief. Sorry, Chief; I must have wandered a bit, Chief."

"By the looks of…THINGS…" Jones said, staring down at the Recruit's rampant uncut cock oozing semen like a fountain, "… it must have been an exciting and happy wandering. Now…" he said, "I want you two, Pete and Alex, to come with me into the shower, and I want EVERYONE ELSE TO GATHER 'ROUND TO OBSERVE AND LEARN HOW TO GIVE A FULL-BODY SHAVE TO YOUR BUNKMATE OR ANYONE ELSE. I've changed my mind, Pete; I'm not going to shave you. You are going to shave Alex first — under my directions, of course — and then, he's going to return the… favor."

"Chieeeeeeef…" you bellyached in disappointment.

He cut you off, saying, "Don't argue. You ARE bunkmates, and you ARE going to do it."

In a metal chest on the floor just outside the largest group-shower room you'd ever seen, Pete — forty heads, no less; do you remember? — were countless cans of Burma Shave shaving lather, and hundreds of experimental, not-yet-marketed, 'just-off-the-assembly-line', disposable razors. [New recruits were to be the 'guinea pigs' on which the new razors were to be tested.] Oh, yes, and several pairs of scissors.

"You'll need some lather, one scissors, and at least four razors — get a handful," ordered Jones. Pete bent over to open the chest and was rewarded with a score of wolf-whistles and a plentitude of bawdry remarks concerning a certain upturned, quaking butt-hole. "Come along, Alex. We have a date with destiny if you do indeed plan to stay in the Navy."

"Chief…?" His anguished appearance and tone merely magnified his distaste of the forthcoming denuding.

Chief Jones chuckled with a grin, seeing the discomfort. "Just think of it as a hazing or initiation into one of your highfalutin' Ivy League college or university fraternities, Alex." After a moment's hesitation in devious thought, he said, "Oh, that's right. Fraternal hazing can be much worse than a mere shaving, can't it? How'd you like a donkey-tail-dildo rammed up your backside whenever you're in barracks? Huh, Alex? Or while on your knees at latrine duty, huh? With your head in the crapper?"

The first week was for the aforementioned 'hurry-up-and-wait' activities, and everything else that goes along with Indoctrination and the obtaining of every piece of your Recruit uniforms (Work and Dress).

That first night would be remembered as the 'Night of Terror'. Long after the designated 'Lights Out', by the Chief's prerogative they remained lit in Barracks 209. Everyone was shaved to a *satisfactory* smoothness, though not a soul was exempt from a dab of styptic pencil for a nick or two or three or four, here and there. Nearly everyone became aroused when a lathered hand slowly slipped up or down or over or around his engorged cock, moving it this way and that, facilitating a better access for the razor to the supposedly tight, targeted skin.

Not surprisingly, Recruit Peabody discovered the pleasures of someone else touching him where no one other than he, himself, had touched since he was a baby. Embarrassed and red-faced, he could not contain himself. His constrained juices plastered your chest and pecs and groin when you tried to stand from your crouched position in front of him.

Turn-about was indeed fair play, and when it was Alex' time to shave you, you coated his chest and face with your own version of bittersweet eggnog.

Things really heated up after Pete and Alex had 'demonstrated' how to shave each other. Somewhere around forty naked Navy Recruits were called into the showers, half to be shaven, the other half to shave. Then the roles were reversed. More 'accidental' climaxes were forth-cumming, and a few brave slippery fingers 'accidentally' slid into hot, puckering, shitty assholes. Afterwards, the remaining Recruits had their turn-abouts. Coincidentally, a few 'brown-noses' suddenly appeared while getting up close and personal while shaving the bunkmates' derrières.

Some were more successful in self-control than others, but not very many. The shower-room began to smell like a bathhouse of orgiastic pleasures with the musky odor of nervous masculine sweat and cum. Thank God, the pipes weren't frozen, or else the water couldn't have washed all the shaved hair and eighty-three uncontrollable offerings of spooge — or perhaps a few less — down the drains and into Lake Michigan. Oh, those lucky fish!

The lights were finally extinguished by 0230 hours, but then at 0430 it was up and at'em and marching began again by 0500 hours.

Then, that second day, after filling your duffle bag with new uniforms, shoes, and heavy boots, rather than immediately taking it back to the barracks, you and the rest of Company 209 had to haul your heavy loads behind your right shoulders [ahhh, such a mental vision!] while marching and running, marching and running, marching and running. A couple of your 'ship mates' [as they were called, even as temporary landlubbers] actually passed out and collapsed from the physical exertion that their lead-asses weren't accustomed to and had to be taken to sick bay.

Every piece of your uniforms had to be folded 'properly', and placed in your combination-locked locker. Your black shoes had to be spit-shined to a mirror finish. Everything had to be placed in your private locker 'just so'. Like the old saying goes, 'There's a time and a place for everything, and everything when not in use, should, at all times, be in its place.'

During that first week, you felt like you'd entered a living Hell. Marching. Marching. And more marching. Cigarette butt detail on the grounds, everywhere. Running. Latrine duty. Sometimes, when on your knees scrubbing the bottoms of the tall urinals — ever wonder why they were so tall? So you could piss through your upright morning hard-ons! — that extend down to the deck, or cleaning around toilets, you'd be teased and humiliated by your raunchy bunkmates about your mouth or ass being available for their service since your body was blocking the specific facility. Then you'd return the humiliation when it was someone else's turn to be scrubbing the facilities. More marching. Training in firefighting. More running. Training in marksmanship. Calisthenics to further develop your strong, graceful body. Running obstacle courses that bordered on extreme gymnastics. Learning and practicing the sports of boxing and wrestling, though... awww shucks!... not in the ancient nude Greek style. Classes in basic and advanced swimming. Occasional 3a.m. full-Company hikes just because a single asshole would not admit some wrongdoing, no matter how minor — and no one would rat him out. Classes in Naval history and regulations. Classes in learning the Semaphore (Flag) Code. And finally, yet still more marching, come rain or come shine or a rare Fall snowstorm. You'd never been more tired in your life while working the farm in Okefenokee. Shit! Catching three- or four-foot gators was child's play compared to Basic Training, and wrastlin' an' hog-tyin' an eight-footer was just about as bad as one o' those twenty-five mile runs. Just about. Your muscles hurt just as bad when it was finished and done with. If not more.

You learned, Pete, that the five ruffians on the bus had been quartered in the brig for a month's duration, and would be assigned to a different Company for one final opportunity to stay in the Navy. *IF* their attitudes had changed. You only wished them the best... the *very* best... new asshole they could get while in there.

Within that month, you'd dropped seventeen pounds, and your six-pack was showing clear indication of becoming an eight-pack, just as Chief Jones said it would. Your smooth thighs, upper arms, and pecs were bulkier... sexier. You'd thrown yourself into everything Chief Jones had ordered, and you'd given him a hundred and ten percent every time he'd come up with anything for you to do. That is... anything except for one thing.

On the evening of your twenty-eighth day, while you were washing off the smoke and ash and odor of your Firefighting Class, Recruit Frank Moore rushed into the showers still wearing his regulation baggy boxers that even a Mormon or a Muslim wouldn't object to, so it didn't appear that he was there for any water sports. "Hey, Pete," he called out above the sounds of the water and the talking; "the Chief wants to see you ASAP... *in his private quarters*. No need to dress; just be decent." That last sentence, delivered in a devilish, high-pitched, effeminate voice, brought a chorus of 'ooooo's' and 'ahhhhh's' from nearly everyone within earshot.

Under the spray of another showerhead, Recruit Jimmy Murphy was lathering himself up generously and slowly stroking his handy playmate. He turned to face you as he pulled his prepuce back as far as it would go, exposing his pee-hole. Softly, he began singing Christy Carlson Romano's lyrics:

> *"Hey (ah ah)*
> *Teachers Pet*
> *I Wanna Be Teachers Pet*
> *I Wanna Be Huddled And Cuddled As Close To You As I Can Get"*

"Aw-rite, smart ass. Where'd y'all learn them words? That week ya done spent at tha State Capital afore ya was a Senior?" you asked as you turned off the water, grabbed a towel, and quickly began drying yourself. "Jes' cut it out; it ain't nuttin' like that." Your reference to his week at the State Capital came from his having told you and a few others about his being appointed to represent his high school by attending Boys State for exposure to governmental and political goings-on.

"Yeah, right!" Jimmy replied. Several others echoed his words, or at least, his sentiments. "We see how you two're always smiling and winking at each other."

"It don't mean nuthin' 'ceptin' he unnerstands me and I unnerstand him."

"Yeah, right!" Jimmy and a couple others replied again.

Having finished drying yourself, you grabbed the diagonally opposing corners of your damp towel, whirled it around a few times, and then snap-popped Jimmy's ass.

"Owwwww!" he let out a yell. "You're gonna get yours, you shit-head," he teased, running after you. You knew you didn't have time to wrap the towel around your waist, so, you held it in front of you to hide your cock and balls, still trying to out-run Jimmy; both of you left wet footprints on the linoleum deck. He reached around you, grabbed the towel and snap-popped you on the ass in retaliation. You kept running, bare-assed naked, toward the locker next to your rack.

"No streaking!" yelled one.

"Get some clothes on, man!" hollered another.

"Wha'sa matteh… Peee-teh? Didja fergit and bend oveh to pick up the soap in tha show'r?" taunted a set of perfect white teeth surrounded by the blackest and shiniest lips you'd ever seen… blacker and shinier, even,

than Darkness. His name — Chakka Zzyzx… no joke! From California.
Strange names there be thar, Matey.

You gave him the middle finger salute, but then gazed at him a
second longer than you should have, and 'Junior' jumped with excitement.
'Damn! He *IS* a gorgeous hunk,' you thought to yourself before saying,
"Shut up, fucker. Chief wants ta see me on tha double."

"Least of all, callin' me that, ya knows where I'd be — fuckin' yer
ass, if ya gimme the chance, but if the Chief wants ta see ya on tha double,
ya be sure to grab yer ankles *REAL* tight!" he yelled back as you hurried into
your baggy skivvies and dashed toward the Chief's door.

Your heart began beating faster, joined by your shallow breaths.
You blushed as you noticed your face warming, your hands and underarms
perspiring, and the tingle in your dingle growing stronger with each hurried
step. The demagogic inculcator of your lust was behind that closed door.

Four steps to go.

Three.

Two.

One.

A damp, bare foot stomped next to its opposite twin. Hands at your
sides, you stopped, composed yourself, threw your shoulders back [your
naked nipples extended another quarter of an inch], took a deep breath,
raised your right fist, and confidently double-knocked twice.

<knock, knock… knock, knock>

"Enter," he mumbled.

CHAPTER FIVE

A new name; first come, first served

The Venetian Blinds were closed behind the windows on either side of the door stopping you from seeing in. You'd heard his call for you to enter. You opened the door and slowly pushed it into Chief Jones's private quarters, then stepped in with caution. Looking around, you saw his bare back as he was facing away from you at his desk. You stood at Attention and said in a strong voice, "Seaman Recruit Dix reportin' as…"

"Cut the crap, Pete. As you can see…" he said, putting down a pencil and closing a folder before turning in the swivel desk chair to look you up and down, "…we're both naked except for our skivvies. It's almost time for lights out, and we don't need any regulation 'Yes, Sir, No, Sir,' shit with just the two of us in here, now, do we? Within these four walls, you can call me 'Davy'. Remember that."

"'D-D-Davy', Sir?"

"Remember…" he said, pointing directly to you, "…you don't call me 'Sir' or 'Chief' until after you leave these quarters, and I don't call you 'Recruit'. I might call you some other names, but not that one. You okay with that, Pete?"

"Yes, suh... uhhh... uhhh... D-Davy." You both gave a good laugh and you said, "I guess ol' habits are hard to beat... uhhh... Davy. Whew! Almos' said sumpin' else."

Jones chuckled again, then said, "D.N. Jones... David N. Jones. Everybody calls me 'David'... *period!* Well, I should say that *only* my *special* friends get to call me 'Davy'... and *only* when not on duty, and I'd like to consider you a friend." Then, without another pause in his words, he went on: "You mentioned old habits are hard to beat."

Still standing, you nodded, shifting your weight, trying to relax.

"Well..." he continued, "...lots of things are hard to beat in a Company of... what is it now... eighty-three young and horny sailors who haven't had any pussy for the past four weeks?"

"Yeahhhhh," you mumbled more out of habit than anything else, as a frown crossed your brow, and you wondered where the conversation was heading.

As he rose from the chair and moved to the small refrigerator under the window nearest the desk, he asked, "How about a beer... off the record, of course... whadoyasay?"

"Uhhh... sure! Whatcha got?"

He squatted down, sorta sideways to you, spread his knees wide, and opened the door all the way so that you could see his stash of cold ones. "Schlitz, Blatz, Pabst, Hamm's, Bush, Bud, Miller, Coors, and Heineken," he rattled off, sounding more like a bartender than a Company Commander.

Your words came soft and slow. "Well, I ain't never hear'd of enny uv'em but Bud an' Millers; either'd be fine by me, Chie... uhhh... Davy," you said as if you were in some kind of trance or something. Your eyes never darted away from staring at the shiny, bullet-shaped cock-head and smooth ball-sack peaking out of the left leg of his skivvies.

"Then let me expose you to a great one from the Netherlands — Heineken — my favorite."

He reached in the fridge, retrieved two bottles of the golden brew, popped off the bottle-cap with his bare fingers, and reached up, handing it to you. It was then that he noticed your tongue was slowly, sexily, moistening your lips. Following your line of sight, he looked down and saw the objects of your interest. Glancing ahead, he must have noticed a movement in your own skivvies.

"Sorry about this," he said, covering his exposed bits as he stood. A little tug of the material and he was decent again, and then he closed the door to the fridge. He turned around and clicked bottles with you.

Before he could say anything else, you said, "It don't bother me none, and... uhhh..." you hesitated from saying what you wanted.

"And... uhhh... what?" he asked, using your tone and phrasing but with a curious glint in his eyes.

Then, Pete, with the feelings you'd harbored for the nearly-naked man standing not more than two feet from you, you took a deep breath and, while once again staring at the tubular mound in his shorts, dared to speak your true hope and desire. "This is your private quarters, Davy. It's where ya live 'n' sleep 'n' do yer paperwork. I've seen ya nekkid before... Hell... ever'body's seen ya nekkid before." You both laughed at that. "So take'em off if ya'd be more ta home. I used ta run around nekkid all tha time in tha swomp. I know how good it feels to let it all hang out."

Your heart was racing with fear, but also with anticipation. Fear that what might just HAPPEN could get you, *and him*, kicked out, but there was also the hopeful anticipation that something MIGHT just happen for the very first time in your life.

He then surprised the shit out of you, eradicating some of the fear, by saying five little words: "I will... if you will." Then he added, "The ball's in your court, Pete."

Well, what the fuck were you guys waiting for? You clicked beers again, set the bottles aside, and as in one 'drill team' maneuver, each of you shed those baggy, ugly, regulation shorts — nothing sexy about them. Where they ended up, you didn't pay attention to, but you both grabbed your bottles and took another deep swig.

"Don't drink it all at once," Jones gulped, shortening his swig. "I'm not letting you have more than one, and we've got lots to talk about tonight. The coffee's on, in the little kitchenette through there." He nodded his head toward another door leading farther back in his quarters, "in case you get thirsty for… for something else."

When he said, "something else," you unconsciously started biting your lips — first, the bottom, then, the top — as you again looked down at his danglies. Instantly, it did a silent little jump upwards, presumably to get a better peak at you and yours with its single 'eye'.

"Have a seat, Pete, either on my bed, which is soft, or the desk chair, which, being solid wood, is kinda hard on the ass." Sorta like you'd seen in the school's football shower-room, he slapped you on your pantless, naked rear-end in what could only be considered as a buddy slap.

"Speakin' frum esperience?" you blurted out.

"YES!" he firmly answered, then broke into laughter. "Sit! Your choice," he ordered.

Well… since he'd reverted to giving orders, you reverted to responding to them. You snapped your naked heels together, tucked your naked ass backwards making your hairless cock and balls swing to and fro, thrust your hairless, naked chest out, nipples alert, your head held high with chin tucked in, and you sharply saluted. "Aye, Aye, Chief!" And you sat in the swively chair with a bare-assed <ker-plop> and took another drink of your Heineken. <Burp> "Oops," you said; "not bad manners; jes good beer."

Jones laughed and let out a huge, long <Burrrrrrp> himself, which got you to laughing. "How's the Heineken?" he asked, sitting on his twin-sized bed and leaning back against one of his two pillows and the wall. He pulled his feet up onto the bed, crossed his legs at the ankles, and let his knees fall to the sides, opening and exposing his thickening fullness to your eyes.

"Good. I like it. It's more… uhhh… I dun know howta… say it."

"Mellow? Soft?"

"Yeah. Both o' those." You turned up the bottle and emptied its golden nectar into your mouth.

"Boy! You sure went through that one kinda fast. I wasn't gonna let you have another, but what the hell? You up for it?" His eyes darted to your heavy-looking crotch and back to your eyes.

"If'n ya thinks it'll be awrite... uhhh... D.J." He was lookin' better every minute, you thought. And li'l ol' 'Omar' was showin' his appreciation for the thoughts that were flooding your mind. A tiny little bit of drool oozed out of his bright pink slit.

Hearing the name 'D.J.', Jones smiled at the memories of Johnny B. Goode (with the 'e' being silent), his best friend in high school. Johnny, too, had called him 'D.J.', and the night before Jones had left for Boot Camp all the way across the continent in San Diego, Johnny had given-up the most private part of his body to the boy-man who would be leaving the next day. But for some reason, they'd never stayed in touch with each other after that night. Such bittersweet memories. Ahhh, yes. Maybe...

In his reverie, Jones's breathing had slowed considerably. For minutes, he said nothing, but his smile grew millimeter by millimeter as he slowly teased his growing tumescence with the side of his thumb, the fingers of his left hand resting on his thigh.

"Davy," you said, trying to get his attention. "You awright, Davy?... David!... CHIEF!"

At that, he was jolted back to the present moment. "Y-Y-Yeah? What's wrong?" he asked, quickly blinking his eyes.

"Ya looked like ya was out of it — starin' straight ahead, a shit-eatin' grin on yer lips. Wuz ya dreamin' with yer eyes open?"

"No. Just thinking about..." He quickly stopped the answer, not wanting to go any further. Then he shook his head to clear it a bit, stood up, and headed toward the fridge, his thick cock leading the way.

"Musta been sumpin' stimulatin', I see," you said. You both chuckled, but he made no comment about what you'd said.

"Now, this is the last one for tonight, Pete," he said, retrieving two more Heinekens. He opened them and handed you one. "Take it easy. Make it last. Sip on it."

'Sip on it, hell!' you thought to yourself. 'Frum what I've seen in books, I'd like ta shuv it in my mouth 'n' swalla tha whole thang 'n' chug-a-lug!' The juicy head of his dick was looking mighty fine to you as you slowly pushed down HARD on the base of your own oozing prick to keep it from exploding in front of your Company Commander. That did the trick — just thinking of who he really was. For the time being, at least.

You accepted the cold Heineken, clicked bottles again, and Jones sat back against the wall almost in a cross-legged 'Lotus' position, opening himself to you once more. "Now, we've got to talk," he said, sounding — albeit not *looking* — like the Chief Petty Officer that he, in fact, was.

You knew it was time to be serious. Sitting up straight in the wooden swivel chair, you slid the sweaty, cold bottle between your thighs and against your crotch, instantly causing li'l Omar to shrink nearly into oblivion.

"Yes, Sir... uhhh... Yes, Chief."

He chuckled to himself but said aloud with a twinkle in his eyes, "I've never had one of these talks... like this," he pointed back and forth several times from his own naked body to yours. Then he became quiet, and you could tell that he was considering exactly what to say. A moment or so later, he began.

"I like you, Pete. You seem intelligent. More intelligent than most of the fuckers who come through Great Lakes, though most of the time you talk like a hick... uhhh... I didn't really mean 'hick'... you talk like a country boy — most of the time. A few times I've heard you talk without your Southern drawl, and used words that even I don't understand, like you were from Yale or Princeton or some other big-city university. You've shown initiative, and I've seen you step in and help other recruits when they were having difficulties. You're quick to learn new things; you take on new assignments without arguing. And I think you're the only one in the entire Company who's already learned the Semaphore Code. I just can't make you out, Pete."

You wet your whistle with another sip of the Heineken, then returned the bottle to your crotch and also to hide your dick. "This conversation has turned serious," you said with none of that country-boy dialect. "Should I call you 'Sir', or 'Chief Jones', or do you still want me to call you 'Davy' or 'D.J.'… while we're in here, I mean?"

"'Davy' is fine," he answered, grinning. "So what gives?"

"Bein' raised as poor as Job's turkey…" you said with just a touch of that delightful twangy dialect, "…I got laughed at a lot. When I first started to school, kids picked on me 'n' made fun of my tight, worn 'n' torn britches that only came to just below my knees. Shoes so tight, Mama had ta cut out the toes so I could wear'em. I learned that if I exaggerated the way I talked, the kids would still laugh, but it weren't a cruel laugh — it wuz like they enjoyed it.

"By the time I wuz in about the sixth grade, I spent a lot of time in the school library, readin' nearly everything in there. Miz Marian DuBois, the librarian, helped me a lot and would order books she thought I might enjoy — books on Scoutin', on the Army, Navy, Marines, an' th'Army Air Corps. Life in Okefenokee wuz easy most o' tha time, but other times, it was damned hard — 'scuse my French, but it wuz."

Jones smiled and nodded that it was okay.

Changing the subject for a minute, you said, "This chair's getting' hard on my butt. Ya mind if I sit over there on the bed with ya, Davy?"

"Not at all, Pete; not at all. Come on over here, buddy." He reached down beside the bed, grabbed another pillow, and held it against the wall. "I think your bottle might be empty, I know mine is. What the fuck! Grab us another couple of cold ones, then come on up here and just lean back an' relax. We're just a couple of buddies here, talkin', and enjoyin' each other's company."

You got up from the chair, stepped over to the fridge, bent from the waist exposing your dark pink little asshole to the Chief, and pulled out two more Heinekens. You stood and handed one to him and plopped down beside him, leaning your back against the pillow that was held against the wall by Jones's hand. But once there, he left his arm behind your back and his hand cupping your right shoulder.

Like him, you pulled up your feet, crossed your legs at the ankles, and let your knees relax out to the sides. But your left knee touched his right knee and you jerked yours back up to avoid the naked contact.

"That's all right," he said. "You can rest your leg on mine." As he said that, he removed his arm from behind your shoulders, put his hand on your left knee, and pushed it back down onto his right one. Then he slid his hand about halfway along the thigh to your crotch. "Your skin's so nice and smooth. I just love to feel naked, shaved skin," he said, sending tingles back through your dingle once more. "DAMN! That is one hellacious scar on your right calf," he said, really noticing it for the first time. He reached over and rubbed his hand across the rough and wrinkled scarring of the skin; quickly it became more like a massage, and as he leaned in more, his elbow was rubbing your once-again rising tumescence.

You put your hand on his forearm to stop the titillating movements, and without looking at him, you asked, "Should you be doing this, Chief? I mean, should *WE* be doin' this?" you corrected yourself.

He removed his arm and hand, and leaned back against his pillow. After some moments, he said, "Look at me, Pete."

You did.

"These rooms back here are my little world. What happens here… stays here. I'll not force you to do anything you don't want to do, and in here, I don't want you doing anything just because you think I, as your Commanding Officer out there…" he pointed toward the Recruits' dormitory, "…want you to do. Ya got that clear, son?"

Since he'd called you 'son', you felt obliged to answer as you did. "Yes, Sir."

His arm returned to behind your shoulders, and as his hand cupped your right shoulder, you felt a little pressure when he eased you over to lean against his smooth, hairless ribcage. It did kinda feel good to you since you'd never had any real male bonding with your drunken step-daddy, and you just relaxed into his tug.

"So, tell me about that scar. Does it hurt when you're marching or running or doing calisthenics or anything?"

"Naw, it don't hurt. It don't hurt a'tall. I wuz about twelve or thirteen when it happened."

"You talking about the alligator I've heard you mention a couple of times?"

"Yep. That's tha one. We wuz out gator huntin'…"

"'We'? Who's 'we'?"

"Well, there wuz my step-daddy an' me, and then there wuz Shadrach an' Darkness."

"Shadrach and Darkness?"

"Yeah; Shadrach's a Colo'ed man, an' Darkness is his son… poorest folk I ever knew… even poorer than we were. Shad (as we called him) an' my step-daddy was part-time gator hunters who worked together, an' they wuz our nearest neighbors down in Okefenok. We could just make out their little shanty across the swomp and through the Cypress trees. Our shack weren't much better."

"And Darkness?"

"Well, he's Shad an' Vashti's son and he and I're tha same age; we wuz both even born on tha same day. 'Cause he was a Darkie, he couldn't go to the school where I went, an' there weren't no Negra schools anywhere around, so, I sorta taught him how to read and write and do his numbers. Oh, he was the blackest person I ever did see… before seein' that Chakka fella, here… but we wuz good friends. An' big! My Lord, he had the biggest… well, let's just say he wuz big… all over!"

That brought about a hearty chuckle from Jones.

"But one day, Shad an' Darkness, and my step-daddy an' me wuz out in our little boat, huntin' for a giant of a gator we'd all heard about. Well, ta make a long story short, we found'im after a few hours, and Daddy threw a rope noose 'round the gator's muzzle, an' MANNNNN! Did he start afightin'!

"I jumped in tha water ta start tyin'im up — I wuz a good swimmer… as long as I could hold my breath. Tha noose wuz 'round his muzzle but i'tweren't real tight, an' his head an' tail wuz athrashin' like crazy, an' his legs an' feet were clawin' at ever'thang in tha water. I jes wuzzn't careful; that's all there wuz to it. He couldn't open his mouth wide enough ta bite through the leg bone, but his front teeth got hold o' my calf muscle. I let out a gurglin' yell under water, an' that's when Darkness jumped in with the God-awfullest Army knife I ever seen, and cut the fucker's throat and then slit his chest frum his throat to his tallywhacker. Shit! Even soft, that gator's tallywhacker was bigger'n the one Darkness hauled around when he was hard up!

"So, then what happened?" Jones asked while he was laughing at your Southe'n expressions.

"Well, he wuz dead by then — tha gator, I mean; not Darkness — and Shad and Darkness got'im up and laid'im across the boat while Daddy tied up my leg with some dirty ol' rags, an' they hurried us over to Vashti and Shad's little shanty. Darkness'es, too. For a Negress, Vashti was... IS... beautiful, and she's kind of a Voodoo doctor, healer, priestess, whatever.

"I'd passed out with tha pain an' tha lettin' o' blood, so I don't know what she done to me, but when I woke up, I wuz layin' on Darkness' hammock; my leg was all bandaged up, and I didn't feel no pain a'tall. I noticed lots o' bottles of Rum all 'round the place, and Vashti told me that whenever I felt any pain, just ta take a swig outta one o' tha bottles I could reach, and that I was NOT to try to walk on my legs until SHE told me I could. And I ain't even gonna tell ya how I took a crap or a piss. It's just too damned embarrassin'. Speakin' uv which..."

At that, Jones suggested they go back to his private bathroom and take a leak. While doing just that, neither tried to hide the fact that they were eyeing each other's... 'equipment'.

"Ho... ho... hold it fo... fo... for me! Quick!" Jones struggled to say as he reached over, grabbed one of your hands, and put it on his pissing cock. In a flash, he grabbed some toilet paper, held it to his face and sneezed — albeit a very fake one — and then blew his nose.

"Oh! Thank you," he said, taking deep, recuperative breaths as he reached over and slid his hand under yours so he could hold your pissing cock. His thumb and index finger held your dick as his other three fingers gently massaged your Balzak... uhhh... 'peter' and ball-sack and dick[s]. "That reminds me..." he said, finishing his piss, removing his hand from your dick (which had just finished doing it's thing), and giving himself a good shake.

"What's that?" you asked, giving yourself a good one.

"Remember I said that we were gonna have to do something about your name?

"Yeah."

Still naked, you and 'Davy' headed back to the other room.

"Well, I've come up with your 'new' name."

"Uh, oh. And just what might that be?" you asked with no drawl whatsoever.

"D.I.X.," he said. "You know your Roman numerals?"

"Yeah," you answered and the 'wheels' started turning.

"D.I.X. is five hundred and nine; right?" You nodded. "Sooooo, while you're in Boot Camp, your new name is gonna be 'Recruit 5-Oh-9'." With an all-knowing attitude, he sat back on the bed and again leaned against the pillow against the wall.

"I like it!" you exclaimed. "It's so... so..."

"Robotic?"

"Yes! Robotic! I like it." You, too, plopped back onto the bed against the other pillow against the wall.

"Good!" he exclaimed. "Now that that's settled, you wanna finish your story?"

"If you're interested."

"I'm interested, '5-Oh-9'." You smiled. He chuckled. "How long did the Voodoo medicine take before you could walk again?"

"About three-and-a-half weeks, but Vashti and Darkness would only let me get up to use the outhouse, and Darkness had to be right by my side to keep me from fallin' if my leg gave out, but it did heal fine. After six weeks, Vashti let me go back home."

"And you don't have any problems with it?" His concern sounded like he'd returned to Company Commander mode again.

"None at all, Chief."

"Interesting story. Did you go back to chasing alligators?"

"I wanted to, and *DID* a couple of times, but Mama insisted that my step-daddy and Shad and Darkness could tend to that stuff; she wanted me to tend to the hogs and the cow and horse, but when the corn and cotton came in, Daddy would help with that."

Outside, or rather, in the dormitory part of the building, *Taps* was heard, signaling 'Lights Out', and on the last note of the bugle call, the lights were extinguished out there except for the Exit signs, which also served as dim nightlights.

"It's getting late," Jones said, "and I've still got a few things I want to discuss with you, '5-Oh-9'. Now do you want to hit the sack, or stay and talk? I can't excuse you from morning exercise, but I can cut you some slack for keeping you up..." he paused, looked into your eyes, then down at your flaccid cock, and back up to your eyes, grinned and wriggled his eyebrows. You blushed, but did nothing other than direct your line of sight to his throbbing, pulsing, dick, which caused a similar response in your own.

"We can keep on atalkin', Davy," you answered, again slipping into your adorable drawl.

"Okay; cutting right to the... *meat*... of the matter," Jones said with a smirk, "how did you learn the Semaphore Code so fast?"

"Well, it really took a while," you replied, scratching a little itch under your balls, "but it wuzznt here; I learned it back in Okefenok, when I wuz laid-up frum tha gator bite."

"How'd you do that?"

"Well, I had Darkness go over an' git a book for me; Mama knew where I kept'em. So then, he an' I learned the Code together. He had a lot more trouble with it than I did, though — his spellin' weren't so good. I taught'im just about ever bit o' book-learnin' he got. I guess I didn't teach him enough, though."

"What'd you boys plan to do with it, once you learned the Code?"

"Well," you began again, "since Shad and Vashti didn't have any electricity or telephones — an' we didn't either — Darkness and I could talk to each other across the swomp by using the Code with our home-made flags."

"You taught him the Code while you were recuperating?"

"As much as I could, but I wuz really jes learnin' it m'self. We got pretty good with it, though."

"I should say." Then after a pause, he said, "We've got to hurry along."

"Yes, Sir." It seemed strange to you to speak formally while sitting there completely naked with your Commanding Officer, but what else were you to say when he used THAT tone of voice?

"So now, tell me… where did you learn all those different steps in marching. I don't recall reading in your files that you were a member of the school band."

"Oh, no, Mister Jones, we couldn't a'ford for me ta be in tha band. I neveh even touched a horn or a drum in my life. But I learned ta march from books, an' then I taught Darkness an' we liked to play soldier when we wuz on dry ground, an' sailor when we wuz on the water on the good ship, Okefenok."

"'Okefenok', huh? What's the difference between 'Okefenok' and 'Okefenokee'?"

"Ohhh," you chuckled. "'Okefenok' is jes one o' tha names folks around there calls it. 'Okefenokee' is tha real name."

"I see. Well, back to you and Darkness, you two were real good friends, weren't you?" he asked, again putting his hand on the naked, warm skin of your thigh, rubbing back and forth a few inches, near but not quite touching the growing tube and tightening sack of your crotch.

"Yeah," you said, looking off into nowhere, "we sorta grew up together — didn't have nobody else to play with. We wuz kinda like brothers even though he wuz Colo'ed and I wuz White."

"Mind if I ask you something… *personal*?"

"Is this sorta 'off tha record', Davy?" you asked, looking him straight in the eye.

"Definitely."

"Then, you can ask ennythang ya want, but I mite not wanna answer ya."

"Fair enough," Jones replied. He removed his hand from your thigh, dropped his left leg off the twin-sized bed, and turned to face you straight on. "Okay, here goes." He took a deep breath, held it for a moment as he bit his lower lip, then gave a big sigh. "Pete... were you and Darkness ever closer than... uhhh... close friends?"

You turned your head and studied him for a bit, trying to understand what exactly it was that he was asking. A series of pictures came to mind — pictures that you had *sacreligiously*, or so you'd been led to believe, allowed yourself to have, to imagine, and yes, to fantasize about, to the point of spontaneous but evilly delightful ejaculation. For a moment, a sense of guilt pervaded your feelings.

During the 'viewing' of those 'pictures', your eyes had dared to leave his, and moved down to the bed. You avoided looking at his obvious nakedness, and only when you felt your own tumescence begin to grow, did you look at your own stimulation.

"No, Sir," you answered truthfully but in a whisper as you turned your head and gazed blindly at the little white refrigerator that became the viewing screen for the playing of your memories.

Neither of you spoke for... who knows how long? But his stare was burning a hole in you, wasn't it, Pete? You knew you had to say something... you WANTED to say something more... but you hesitated exposing your innermost feelings and memories.

Memories of that last afternoon... alone but together... with the Manatees... and each other... lying on the grassy 'beach'... under the blazing sun... sweating... slowly wiping the sweat from each other's naked body... then, wrastlin' and rubbin' your nekkid bodies together... *completely* nekkid together, skin to skin, for the first time ever... havin' feelin's ya'd never had before... wantin' to kiss and taste those full, soft, dark lips, but not permittin' yourself... wrappin' your arms around his back and bringin' his head down to your shoulder... then biting his neck 'n' tastin' a little of his blood as your steel-hard penis exploded its white-hot juices, again and again, between your rigid bodies... discovering that he had done the same thing as he yelled in pain and ecstasy... panting for renewed breath... calming down... feelin' guilty... rolling apart and silently entering the Manatees' world again to wash off those sticky juices.

... and not sayin' a word to each other until that final... *"Good-bye."*

A salty tear of remembrance trickled its way down your cheek and worked its way into the corner of your mouth; the taste was bittersweet. It didn't really matter that the Chief had seen it.

"But you wanted to be closer than just friends; didn't you, *son?*" David, Davy, D.J., Mr. Jones, Chief, Chief Petty Officer, Company Commander Jones asked. Suddenly, with that one word spoken with compassion, he had become a father-figure, albeit if only for a few moments. And he didn't ask the question in a condemning way, in a judgmental tone, nor with an interrogating attitude. He asked with concern and care and kindness in his voice.

Without looking up, you simply nodded your head in the affirmative.

"Let's go back and get a cup or coffee. Or would you prefer tea?" he asked, changing the subject as he placed a tender hand on your shoulder.

The two of you were sitting at the tiny kitchen table, having donned the skivvies you'd both shed earlier. He was sipping his black coffee, even though it wasn't coffee *per se*, but rather, roasted chicory. You didn't care for the flavor, so he'd brewed some sweet-tasting sassafras tea. In a way, it made you think of the *comforts*, if you will, of home, sitting there in your underwear you'd picked up and put on before going back to the kitchenette. Coffee was too expensive and the sassafras saplings grew in abundant clusters in Okefenokee Swamp. It tasted similar to Root Beer; some tasted a little like Licorice, and there was nothing like it for soothing a sore throat. And the boiled dried bark DID help to relax you, providing a good night's sleep.

"Pete... how tall are you?" he asked out of the 'blue', without any 'giveaway' expression on his face.

"Five feet, ten-and-a-half inches, Sir."

"Cut the 'Sir' shit!" he said, holding his hand up.

"All right, fucker!" you replied, surprising the holy crap outta him, using that term.

But just as quickly, he countered with, "You're asking for it, aren'tcha?"

You shook your head indicating the negative, and said, "We'll see who bends over first."

That, too, surprised Jones for a moment. But then, getting up to refill the cups, he said, "I WAS gonna offer you a proposition but..."

Jumping to your feet, you teasingly asked, "YOU WERE GONNA PROPOSITION ME, CHIEF?"

"Shut the fuck up, you fucker; ya wanna wake up everybody out there?" he yelled in a raspy whisper, pointing to the dormitory. Yelled a raspy whisper? Now go figure that one out, if you will.

"Gotcha!" was your simple but playful comeback.

"Gotchu!" was his retort just before he grabbed your shoulders, pulled your bare chest tightly against his own, and covered your mouth with his open lips.

Stunned with an overshadowing of weakness, you didn't do anything at first; it felt so good, so warm, so... so...

It didn't take long before 'Omar' was begging for some attention, too, and suddenly you felt 'li'l Jonesy' responding.

Quickly, you pushed away at arms length.

"You wanted this with Darkness; didn't you, Pete?"

Hesitating to answer, you finally said in a quivering voice, "But it would have been wrong."

"Says who?"

"Mama, an' tha Preacherman."

"And where did they get their information?

"I guess frum tha Church an' tha Bible."

"Yep, you're right about that, but you want to know something that not many people realize because their Preachermen, Ministers, Priests, and Bishops don't tell'em?"

"Yeah. What's that?"

"Jesus never condemned men loving men, and He never condemned men lying down with other men as they would with women because it's physically impossible. But it was Saul, who changed his name to Paul, who condemned those things, but when traveling away from home, went everywhere with a young man named Timothy, and who was anti-women in nearly everything. Even Jesus ran around with twelve other men and loved John more than his own brother, if you get what I mean."

"I didn't know that," you said, looking away, thinking. After a moment, you looked back into Davy's eyes and asked, "It woulda been awright, then?"

"Is friendship wrong?"

"Course not."

"Is love wrong?"

"No way!"

"Is kindness and doing unto others as you'd like them to do to you, wrong?"

"Not at all. That's what we're told to do. It's tha Golden Rule."

"Then you just answered your own question, Pete."

You'd relaxed your straight-arming and let Davy drew you to himself again, and he kissed you like you'd never been kissed before. Then he said, "Sit down and finish your tea. I've got something else to tell you."

In a light daze, you sat; you sipped the familiar-tasting tea; you pondered the things you'd just learned. Your whole world was turning upside down. But it felt good — emptyin' out the old shit. "Where'd you learn that from?" you asked, without your Southe'n drawl.

"From MY dad — he was a minister. He preached straight from the four Gospels and the Book of the Acts of the Apostles. He told his congregations to read those books in the red-letter editions, because the red-lettered words were the words of Jesus the Christ, for whom Christianity is named, and not for someone else."

"Wow!" is all you could say.

"It's getting late." He looked at the clock on the wall above your head and said, "It's after midnight, but before you go back to your rack, I want to share something else with you."

You opened your mouth to say something, but he held up his hand to stop you.

"Tomorrow morning... uhhh... this morning... later today, I'm going to announce that I'm making you RLPO... Recruit Leader Petty Officer, and you'll be in charge of marching, when and where, AND it'll be your responsibility to see that everyone in the Company learns the Semaphore Code. If you say such-and-such a recruit knows it, then he'll get weekend passes for the rest of Basic Training. But if you say he knows it and I find out that he doesn't... your ass is going to the Brig. You hear me, Recruit 5-Oh-9?"

"Uhhh... Yesssss Sirrrrr," you said, jumping to an almost naked Attention and saluted.

"And later today, I'm going to TRY to talk with someone, pull a few strings, and get you into the Official Great Lakes Naval Training Center Drill Team, and you'll be performing in your own graduation ceremonies."

"Oh, Chief; I don't know how to thank you. Being in the Drill Team is a dream come true." Your impulse was to rush over to him (even though it wasn't more than three steps) and give him a great big hug.

Before you could say or do anything else, he gave you another set of orders. "Now stand at ease, relax, and come here."

As he issued the orders, you obeyed them. Soon, you were in his arms again, being kissed and kissing back in return. (Great minds think alike.) Very soon, the hardness inside your skivvies was pressed against and rubbing the hardness inside his skivvies. Then, he said, "Stand on top of my feet."

Instead of obeying, you stepped back a step and frowned at him. "Just do it!" he demanded.

Two average sized cut cocks immediately became airborne as they escaped their tented flies and tried to reach each other.

And you obeyed his command to stand on the top of his feet, thereby forcing the two excited members together.

Holding you tightly against himself, he turned off the lights in the small kitchenette. Then he waddled into another room, and without turning on any other lights, continued until the backs of your legs felt something soft. Gently, he lay you on the bed, your legs hanging off the side, and he moved you back, still kissing you. You spread your legs a little wider.

The weight of his torso was on yours, yet at the same time, it felt manly — solid and strong, but not heavy — it felt like a feather — weightless. Your nipples grew hard and extended beneath his smooth, hairless skin — they were scintillating.

His cock rubbing yours; your cock rubbing his; his fingertips exploring every inch of your arms and underarms, your sides and the slightly squished-out ass cheeks.

He broke the tongue-dueled kiss and slid a few inches down your own smooth chest and abdominals; his moist cock (was that pre-cum?) tickled the underside of your balls again and again as he rocked his body up and down your own body. His hands reached up and you sucked after his fingers like a hungry puppy seeking out his dinner. Then you stopped and your hands pulled his hands and fingers away from your mouth.

"If you don't stop soon," you cried with desperation, "my milk's gonna get us both wet. Please stop," you begged.

"I'll stop... right after this," he said, sliding down until his knees were resting on the floor. His right hand held the base of your throbbing 'talleywhacker', and his left hand massaged and rubbed and gently pulled on your 'Balzak'. His moist lips kissed the one-eyed head that the short extra skin had uncovered; then, driving you out of your mind, they slipped all the way down to your pubis. You'd never felt such exquisite torture in your life, Pete, and by the sounds rising from your deepest reactions, he knew you were enjoying it. You felt like you were floating, and for a moment, all you could see was the blackness of space — like black velvet sprinkled with myriads of variously-colored diamonds, each point of light the heart of a firecracker ready to explode.

He pulled harder on your balls and raised his slick lips only to the frenulum. Your breathing quickened and became more anxious. You tensed. You gripped the blanket with your fists. From the muscles in your forehead to the muscles in your smallest toe, you became rigid. Quickly, he descended again, engulfing your entire tumescence. You screamed — a sound that cannot be written, a sound of joy and happiness and excitement and unrequited love you'd never before experienced, a feeling caused by another man's lips and throat! He had swallowed the entirety of the same sweet, yet salty, 'milk' that only once had you ever actually dared to taste just a drop, from your own manipulations, on an island in the swamp, away from home, and even away from Darkness. A wise old owl had looked on from its perch in a nearby Cypress Tree and asked, "Whooo?"

In the darkness of the night and the room, your male essence poured, spurted, and gushed, again and again, until, finally, it merely dribbled out. Already lying down, it felt as if you'd collapsed, exhausted, into the feather-mattress on which you were lying.

Davy, too, had expelled his male essence, but onto the floor and the frame of the bed. He, too, rested — his cheek and almost-non-existent sideburn lying on your crotch — regaining his breath. Then, once more, he slid up your body and kissed you, chastely, not knowing whether you'd object to the taste of semen in his mouth.

But *your* tongue slid through his closed lips, teased his teeth to open, and began a lovers' duel with *his* tongue, surprisingly realizing that you could taste your own essence. Then you acted as if you were greedy, wanting more, from the tangy, slippery lining in his throat. You nearly bruised your lips... AND HIS... gripping the back of his head so tightly and forcing your mouths together so... so... I don't know the word to use. But you get the picture.

CHAPTER SIX

Promotions; Bribes for Liberty Passes

AUTHOR'S NOTE: If you haven't guessed by now, the name, "Omar", is Pete's affectionate name for his favorite playmate who usually hangs, dribbling a drop here and perhaps a drop there, between his legs — usually, but not always. Though I love the Persian poetry in THE RUBÁIYÁT OF OMAR KHAYYÁM (whose name literally means "Omar the Tentmaker"), the expression has long been vulgarized and come into The Urban Dictionary's meaning: "A slang expression for a person experiencing an erection that raises the cloth (trousers or sheet) covering his genitals much like a tent." Pete would also include 'drawers' or other undergarment as another 'cloth' in that explanation.

In THE RUBÁIYÁT's Stanza 51 we read:

> The Moving Finger writes; and, having writ,
> Moves on: nor all thy Piety nor Wit
> Shall lure it back to cancel half a Line,
> Nor all thy Tears wash out a Word of it.

And from Stanza 65:

> Then said another with a long-drawn Sigh,

"My Clay with long oblivion is gone dry:
But, fill me with the old familiar Juice,
Methinks I might recover by-and-bye!"

Use your own creative imagination in order to understand that author's meaning.

And now, enjoy...

The next day was Sunday, a day of rest, 'for the un-wicked', so they say, the only day of the week that allowed you or any of the recruits to sleep in, provided, that is, that you or they were not in the habit of attending Mass or other religious services. Actually, the saying is, 'no rest for the wicked', so... a day of rest *would* be 'for the un-wicked', would it not? Such logic! <tsk>

After the prior evening's climactic conclusion, you felt you really needed the shut-eye when you automatically opened them at 0430 hours. You rolled over, gave your thick, stiff piss-hard-on a couple of slow, sensual, firm strokes and, as Floyd Reginald Alexander Peabody the Third would say... 'returned to the arms of Morpheus'.

But for only a moment, though, because *His Royal Highness*, F.R.A. Peabody III quietly leaned over and tapped your shoulder. "Dix," he said so softly it didn't disturb your slumber. "Dix," he called again, a little louder, as he shook your shoulder a bit more strongly; but still, you gave no response.

"DIX!" he nearly yelled, shaking and waking you suddenly to what you thought might be an unknown-magnitude earthquake.

"Wha... Wha... What's hap'nin'? What's goin' on?" You sat bolt upright, pushed off the sheet, threw your legs over the edge of the rack, and jumped up, almost hitting your head on the metal frame of the upper rack.

Peabody's eyes bulged at seeing your enlarged joystick as he quickly straightened up, drawing back just a bit.

Byron Sweetwater, a Carolina Cherokee, rushed by but came to a sudden halt and looked back, his eyes also riveted to the sight. "Whoa, there, Kemosabe." In a deep voice, playing with White-man's stereotypical Indian dialect, he then said, "Mighty dangerous weapon you got there. Might want to put on loin cloth." He looked toward the front of the barracks. "Hey-yahhhhhhhhh," he called out to his sidekick. "Hank... Hank Snow... come see Peter Dix' piss-tol weapon."

You looked down to see Omar, your naked morning companion. 'OH, MY GOD!' you thought to yourself. Your hands flew to cover your hard-on, but you had to use your right hand for something else. Frantically, you looked through the sheets for your skivvies. Not finding them, you dropped to all fours so you could search under the rack, and by doing so, exposed your bare ass and dangling balls to the three sailors nearby. 'SHIT! I musta left'em in Chief's quarters when I left,' you suddenly realized.

"Ewwwww," chorused the three... no, four... no, five guys, who were then standing around, drawing attention from yet others to the commotion.

"Get dressed," said one.

"At least, put your skivvies on," Hank said as he sauntered by.

"I'm outta here," said a third as he left in an embarrassed hurry.

You jumped up as fast as you could, spun the dial back and forth on your combination lock. "Goddammitalltohell, muther-fuckin' sonuvabitch," you cursed aloud when the lock wouldn't open. You spun the combination again — more carefully — then yanked open your locker, retrieved a clean pair of ultra-baggy shorts, and bent over AGAIN to step into them.

"Lemme know when you're gonna take a shower, Dix," Hank teased. "I'll make sure to drop the soap over close to ya so ya can pick it up."

"Fuck you!" you yelled back.

"I. don't. think. so," came his drawn-out riposte. "But turn-about *IS* fair play, I guess," he said with a twinkle in his eyes.

While all that was going on, Sweetwater teased, "Kemosabe not in rack at Lights Out. Do naked monkey-dance with Big Chief last night... No?" Then he giggled like a Warrior's Two-Spirited wife, as he and Hank left the scene.

Soon, everyone had gone about his own business, everyone, that is, except for Peabody-3.

"What's on yer mind, Peabody?" you asked as a yawn and a stretch seemed to take over your body.

"A little while ago, I, too, had a... uhhh... an enlightening... *session* with Chief Jones in his quarters," he said, letting you know that he knew that you'd talked with Jones in his quarters the night before.

At that bit of knowledge, you became completely awake, standing there, eager to hear what else, if anything, he had to say, and by all indications, there would definitely be more to come.

Peabody continued. "He told me about the things you and he discussed last night."

'Just how much did he tell?' you nervously wondered as you scratched the ring finger of your right hand.

"He told me that tomorrow he's going to announce that he will be promoting you to RLPO [Recruit Leader Petty Officer] and that he'll be promoting me to RCPO [Recruit Chief Petty Officer]," Alex said. "And since you and I will be working so closely together, he told me about you teaching the Semaphore Code and awarding or withholding Liberty Passes. Also about your being in charge of the marching and your joining the Drill Team."

"Is that all he told you, Alex?" you asked, using his *familiar* rather than *formal* name. A very slight, all-knowing grin crept across his usually expressionless face. Dread and a guilty sense of betrayal gripped your guts. A sudden chill seemed to pour over your scalp and all the way down to your nuts.

"Uhhh... Oh! And he told me it would be all right to let you know that we had talked."

You released a sigh of relief as you sank to sit on the edge of your unmade rack. There was no foreseeable reason for him to lie. Things were warming up.

Looking around, seeing that everyone else had apparently left the barracks, Alex stepped closer. The toes of his shoes almost touched the toes of your naked feet. His crotch was not far from your face. You leaned back, taken aback, as it were. He looked around again for good measure and then reached in his pants pocket and pulled out a balled-up piece of ecru-colored cotton material.

"Here," he said, just above a whisper. "I picked this up from under the edge of Davy's bed. It has your name stenciled inside the back of the waistband. I have *NO* idea how they got there," he snickered and wriggled his brow as he handed them to you.

You unrolled the wad of fabric and saw immediately that it was, indeed, your own skivvies you'd dropped to the floor... NO! You *hadn't* dropped them to the floor! Vaguely you remembered... Davy was sliding them off your hips while he was sending you to Heavenly, blissful Nirvana. He must have kicked them aside, and then when he finished and told you to go back to your own bunk while it was still dark, you were so satisfied and so tired, you thought nothing of walking naked through the dark barracks. Or *had* you worn them back? You'd been too sleepy to remember.

"How'd you get'em?" you asked softly after you, yourself, perused the emptiness of the barracks.

"Oh, I'll never tell," he said teasingly, "but *probably* it was the same way mine ended up there, too." He grinned a huge grin as you glared at him, while shoving yours under the pillow. "You don't have to worry, Pete. I'm not going to say anything to anyone. And I trust you won't say anything to anyone about what I just said."

That was when YOUR eyes bulged as you jerked your head up to gaze into HIS eyes. Silently questioning, your index finger pointed straight at Alex, and then you thumbed toward the Chief's quarters. He barely nodded his head, but his sultry, droopy eyelids and his licking his lips told you what his true feelings were. He wanted the Chief. He also pushed down and readjusted the growing bulge in his pants... only inches from your face.

You reached out with both hands, grabbed him by the hips and urged him backward so that you could stand up from sitting on your rack. "Thank you, Alex. I could hug you, but for now, let me just shake your hand." They did. "I owe ya one, buddy."

"That you do, RLPO; that you do. Like I said earlier... I'm above you..." he patted the rack above yours, "...and you're under me. You'll pay," he said with a better-than-thou attitude — one like his daddy might use in Congress or on Wall Street. Then he slowly winked… once. "But I'll go easy on you." And he smiled. "I'll start with one greasy finger."

As usual, *Reveille* was sounded at 0430 hours Monday morning. Bare feet thundered on the linoleum-covered wooden deck of the barracks as eighty-three recruits scrambled from their upper or lower racks. Within seconds, naked morning piss hard-ons bumped against naked legs or ass-cheeks, or dribbled on the rushing comrades vying for an available urinal or showerhead; some even doubled up — close but not touching — at one or the other. You had, however, noticed that those who DID double up were usually quite chummy or buddy-buddy with each other whenever possible.

After those first few mornings of shock, several weeks earlier, no one bothered to complain any longer about standing in someone else's piss in the shower. Everybody did it at home in the privacy of their own tub or shower, but there, it was their own piss in which they were standing. Besides that, a rumor had circulated that urine was a sterile disinfectant, and some of the jocks who'd had bad cases of Athlete's Foot in high school, were beginning to proclaim that it was healing their itchy feet.

The rumor was based on fact, though, for in a later hygiene class, they would learn that POWs of WWII did, in fact, use urine as a disinfectant *AND* as a source of liquid nourishment to stave off dehydration. People do many so-called *weird*, unusual things in order to stay alive when they have to. Embarrassing, disgusting, sacrilegious, inappropriate, evil, WRONG though it was considered by many, in ONE later class it would be discussed that semen, too, is sterile, and primarily consisted of nutritious protein.

Rollo Burnside, a heavyset stud who was one of those above-mentioned high school jocks, and whose arms and legs were at least twice as bulky as anyone else's, proved just how secure he was in his own sexual identity that Monday morning.

"Come on, men; let's see if this rumor's true or false, once and for all. Everyone here in the shower, form a circle around and piss on my feet."

The others were shocked at his request, and the words "fagot," "queer," "golden shower queen," and others flew around the room like the spray from the showerheads; a few included some rather descriptive names of internal body-passages.

"All right, you assholes," Rollo threw it right back at them, "I ain't lookin' for a lover. We're all brothers here in 209, a unit, a team. My feet itch," he said bringing one foot up into his groin and scratching between his toes. "Just do it!"

"Git bot legs in de air, spread'em, an' this cockson'll scratch yo itch goooood," said a bad-ass dark brown dude holding his fat, meaty, black 'baseball bat' already drooling creamy white cock-snot from his brownish-purple portobello-like mushroom head. You'd never seen one like that one, Pete, and truth be known, you hoped you'd never see one like it again. It gave you the willies just to look at it, it was so gross. You couldn't imagine anyone — male OR female — enjoying it. The Latino sounded like he was from the Bronx, and his family name, *Keskeskeck,* indicated his Native American heritage from the same area, though you doubted that he even knew about that side of his family.

"Just try it, and you'll make my day," Rollo said, with a seductive smile that instantly morphed into an angry glare. "POW! Right in the kisser!" he added, throwing his balled-up right fist into his catcher's mit of a left hand.

"OKAY, LADIES! NO BEATIN' ON… or 'OFF'… EACH OTHER IN THE SHOWERS, OR ANY WHERE ELSE," Chief Jones unexpectedly yelled as he walked past. Nearly everyone there turned and snapped to naked Attention at the sound of his voice. Flaccid cocks were swinging like pendulums. Turgid ones — standing tall. And swollen ones — showing the way to proceed — pointing forward.

"YOU GOT FIVE MINUTES TO BE DRESSED IN YOUR FATIGUES AND IN MARCHING FORMATION ON THE BARRACKS QUAD," he continued yelling before he completely stopped, backed up, and looked around the corner at all the different 'cuts of meat' in the showers. "Thanks for all the little salutes," he said, smiling as he glanced into the faces of the men. "I'll remember each and every one of you. NOW, ON THE DOUBLE, YOU COCKSUCKIN' PANSIES!" And at that, he was gone.

"Aye, aye, Chief!" hailed the naked recruits in the shower, or at the sinks shaving, or at the urinals pissing, or on the crappers... doing whatever nature required.

"Is he? Or isn't he?" the whispers and thoughts flew around the room as the showers were turned off.

◇◇◇

And so it went.

As promised, Chief Jones made the announcements that you, Pete, would be the new RLPO [keyword: *Leader*], and Alex Peabody III would be the new RCPO [keyword: *Chief*]. He also told them that you would be responsible for their learning the Semaphore Code, and would award Liberty Passes to those who proved to you that they knew it. He [Jones] also announced that from that moment on, through graduation, you, Pete, would be known as 'Recruit 5-Oh-9'. And he suggested that everyone ask YOU for the meaning of your new name when they came to demonstrate their knowledge of Semaphore.

After morning chow, you led the Company through an hour [fifty minutes, actually] of calisthenics. Then, there were ten minutes of rest followed by a figure-eight five-mile run through an obstacle course. A course of greater difficulty, each week, would follow until graduation. A thirty-minute break for shit & piss relief came next, then drink some water, gobble some peanut butter & cheese crackers [or other light snack], and then head to the hospital basement for swimming instructions / exercises / techniques / endurance training. Once a week, there were classes in using snorkeling and scuba gear for those sailors who'd never used it before — which was the greater majority of the Company. After the noon chow-time, there were different classes every day.

Following evening chow at 1730 hours [5:30 p.m.], you had all of three hours of R&R — that's Rest and Relaxation — in which to take care of your personal laundry, study and go over the day's lessons with a buddy or in a group, spit-shine your marching boots... AGAIN... shit, shower, shave, and shampoo for the second and final time that day, and maybe... just maybe... you felt the need to spank the ol' monkey and empty those pent-up balls of yours.

'To hell with it,' you'd think to yourself. Then you'd do the best you could to turn your back to as many in the shower as possible in order to gain some sense of privacy. You stroked your cock and tickled your balls and diddled your taint — or farther back if you happened to be completely alone in the shower — but you were too fuckin' tired from the day's activities; Omar just would not rise to the occasion. With the hot water spraying down your back, you leaned your forehead against the tiled shower wall in front of you. The hot water was flowing down your aching back and your *not-so-interested* ass-crack. You lathered your hands up real good, grabbed your ball-sack with your left hand and your dangling cock with your slippery right hand, and began slowly stroking him [Omar, that is].

It felt so good and soon you were in a world of your own, totally oblivious to anything going on or being said around you. Faster and faster you went. Harder and harder you worked. And then with a mighty exhalation of defeat, you stopped and returned to the present. "**FUCK!**" you screamed, feeling like you were going to collapse onto the pissy floor — not from any overpowering release, but from exhaustion and the thought that the Navy had stripped you of your manhood.

"It's the Saltpeter [2] they put in the food every day," Byron Sweetwater said, patting you on the shoulder as he stepped into the spray of the showerhead next to you.

You hadn't been aware that he'd entered the shower. You turned to face him, head-on, your hands still gripping your 'jewels' as they had been, but without any movement whatsoever. Your dick was pointing right straight at Byron. "Salt... whut?" you inquired in your cute li'l ol' drawl, looking as innocent as a 'possum sticking his head out from under a branch of a magnolia tree.

"Saltpeter."

"Is that part uv tha word? Or wuz you sayin' my name?"

"Part of the word."

"Whut's that?" you asked with a frown, drawing out the last simple word into three complex syllables. "I never heard o' that."

"Po-tassium ni-trate," he accentuated the positive, correct pronunciation. "It's supposed to keep us guys from getting all horned-up for the twelve weeks of Boot Camp. No telling how many of us would turn queer with no juicy couchie or stinky poontang if we all showed up in the showers with hard-ons… 'specially when someone walks in an' sees a guy…" he looked down at your right hip, "… bent over a bit, with his head against the wall, an' his butt-hole stickin' out so anybody'd have access to it." He wriggled his forehead as he tried to get another glimpse of your behind. "Like my grandfather told me when I entered manhood… 'A stiff dick has no mind of its own; a hole is a hole is a hole… female, male, sheep, or knot-hole in the outhouse. Build a fire there — in your mind — and then use your man-pipe to put it out'."

"Rite," you said, chuckling to yourself at hearing so many of the words and expressions that Darkness had used so often. "Well, I'm all finished in here. Thanks for the lesson, Sweetcheeks… errr… Sweetwater, I mean."

"HEY!" he yelled at you. "Just watch who you're sweet-talking to, or ya might just end up getting' more than you're askin' for."

You grabbed a towel just outside the open shower-room and began drying off.

"Oh, there you are, RLPO 5-Oh-9," came the *charming*, upper-class voice of 'RCPO-III', as you were beginning to think of him. "Naked as usual, I see," he added with a teasingly, smart-alecky tone.

"Wanna dry my back fer me?" you asked him.

"I wouldn't want you thinking that I was trying to bribe you for something, so I'm going to have to say 'No,' to your… uhhh… *proposition*."

"'*Proposition*,' my hind-end!" you exclaimed quite a bit louder than was absolutely necessary.

"Exactly!" RCPO Peabody said rather softly and with a shit-eating grin.

<*Tsk,*> propelled from your tongue and lips; disgustedly, you shook your head. Holding one corner of the towel, you threw the rest of it over your shoulder, grabbed the lowest corner with your other hand behind you, and

began drying your own back. Omar and his two hairless cousins were just hanging around, doing nothing exciting, awaiting their turns at stimulation.

"What kin I do fer ya, Peabody?"

"When can I get my weekend Liberty Pass?"

"Y'all'll have ta talk with tha Chief 'bout that, but I gotta give ya tha permission. Do ya know yer Semaphore?"

"Yes."

"Show me, an' call out each letter as ya do it," you told him as you continued to dry yourself.

"Right here?"

"Whut betteh place?"

And show you, he did… straight through the alphabet from Alpha to Zulu, and not even hesitating with the problem letters, Juliet and Yankee. As soon as you dried off, you went to your locker, donned some clean skivvies, and signed an approval slip for the little 'Chief' to give to the big 'Chief'. "You're my first approval, Alex. I'm proud uv ya. Give this to the Chief," you said, handing him the chit, "and he'll give ya yer Liberty Pass, an' maybe, sumpun' else." You winked at'im.

◇◇◇

For the next few days, it seemed as if everyone wanted your time to show you that they knew the Semaphore Code. You decided to ask RCPO Alex for HIS assistance in examining the Company's knowledge of the code. Most of them were given their chits for the Passes, but a few tried to bribe both you and Alex.

"I'll spit-shine your boots every night, or do your laundry, or buy your cigarettes if you'll just tell the Chief I'm okay." "I'll learn the Code before graduation, I promise," said a couple of the slower recruits.

You knew by what you'd seen that they *were* slow learners, and your heart went out to them, but you didn't want to end up in the brig as Jones had promised if you said they did, but they didn't. Duh! You know what I mean.

Subsequently, both you and Alex worked with them over the day of rest, not using your own passes since neither of you knew any place to go that was near USNTC or down around Chicago or up in Waukegan, and the two slow learners were given their chits the following Monday.

Then on Tuesday, Pacheco Keskeskeck, the Latino dude we talked about earlier, came abeggin', not quite on his knees, but he surprised the shit outta you when he actually, blatantly, no-holes-barred, offered to give you a blowjob if you'd just tell Jones that he qualified for his Liberty Pass. When you said, 'No,' he added a rim job to his offer. After a second 'No,' he even went so far as to say that he'd let you fuck his ass.

Remembering the group-shower incident with big jock Rollo Burnside telling everyone to piss on his itchy feet, you suggested that Pacheco get Rollo to teach him the Code. "The big guy was the third one in the Company to learn it, and he's helped a few others get their Passes," you said.

"He'd nevah do dat fir me... not afta whut..."

"I know what happened and what you said, Pacheco. But he just might surprise you. Talk to'im; he might take you up on your offers... OR he might do it just because he's a nice guy underneath all that jock-beef-cake."

CHAPTER SEVEN

One more time; promises, promises

Your first six weeks at Great Lakes Naval Training Center had come and gone — half of your Basic Training; it took that long to break-in your marching boots, heal the blisters on your heels and big toes, and toughen the soles of your feet. The muscles in your body had daily cried out for relief, and after the first couple of weeks, you rather became numb to the aches and pains too numerous to mention. You reasoned that anyone who loved the physical pain and torture of the training surely would be leaning a bit toward the sadomasochistic way of life.

And... *you...* loved it. No, you didn't just love it... you *thrived* on it. The Chain of Command. The regimentation. The orderliness and discipline. The strict rules. Getting down and dirty, crawling on your belly in full cammies one day or fatigues the next, carrying your *piece* [rifle] in one hand as your other helped you maneuver under the barbed-wire ceiling barely eighteen inches above the dirt. Real, live bullets whizzing past, only inches above the barbed-wire. Doing a hundred and fifty sit-ups with a buddy sitting on your lower legs, facing you, urging you on. "Come on. You can do it. Just one more. You can do it. Gimme one more. One more. One more." On and on — endlessly on. Sometimes, his bulge, or yours, or both, began to grow, making it harder... no... making it more *difficult* to continue. Then, straining to swim fifty laps in the pool in the basement of the hospital — you'd finally learned to coordinate your breathing with the breast-stroke. A hundred pull-ups at a time in the gym. You even got into tumbling and gymnastic routines — the still rings, pommel horse, floor exercise, vault, parallel bars, and the high bar — THOSE, you really enjoyed; it seemed you were a natural at them. Of course, it brought back memories of you and Darkness playing 'Tarzan' (neither of you wanted to be Jane), when you'd cut a Muscadine or Scuppernong vine close to the ground, and then 'fly' with the greatest of ease from tree to tree over the gator-infested waters of the Okefenokee. Daring, but fun. Oh, yes. And dangerous, too, but not as dangerous, you figured, as green recruits crawling under live ammo. Oh, no. Not at all.

You were in decent *farm-hand* shape when you enlisted, but in just six weeks, you'd lost twenty-seven pounds, your skin glowed with good health, and your hard muscles and abs rippled with new-found life — life you never knew you had in you.

Those had been timeless weeks, in that during the passing days, it seemed they would never end, but at Lights Out each night, you and your barracks-mates often wondered if each of you had come awake just before the morning light. "Are we hittin' the rack? Or are we just getting up before the Sun, for some more fuckin' marchin'?" you'd heard more than once from a sailor sitting on the edge of the bottom rack in nothing but his skivvies, elbows on his knees, and his chin cupped in the palms of his hands, too tired to realize the time of day or night. From one perspective, the day never seemed to end, but from another, it had mercifully flown by so fast, you couldn't remember everything you'd done.

With the help of jock-stud Rollo Burnside and RCPO Alex Peabody, you'd finally been able to approve Liberty Passes for everyone in the Company. Yes, even the Latino dude, Pacheco Keskeskeck. Strange as it seems, Pacheco and Rollo had become side-kicks, kissin' cousin's, whatever you wanted to call them; they never seemed to be far apart. Where one was, you could be sure that the other was not far behind, even in the showers. But we'll say no more about that, except for this: at least, they practiced 'turn about is fair play'. In all ways!

Then, as RLPO, you no longer had to teach the Semaphore Code; you only had to Lead the marching exercises with the occasional — still in formation — Company run-throughs of the Code.

And yet, you were so tired, you couldn't even drop a load, no matter how hard you tried, no matter how soft you caressed, no matter how tender you titillated or tickled that 'tingle in your dingle'. 'They must still be feedin' us that Saltpeter,' you thought to yourself many a time.

But on Sunday evenings, when the guys came back from Liberty, they all talked about "what a fucking good time" they had had with the hookers in Waukegan, only four short, horny miles from the Base. But you learned very quickly to take their bragging with a grain of salt. They were probably returning just as virgin as they'd been when they signed out. It was the quiet ones you wondered about, though. And their sly, almost non-existent smiles as they kept to their own thoughts and memories. 'Sailors together???' you wondered, 'Or did they get a cure for that Hawaiian disease that every recruit had... Lack-o'-nookie?'

But then you remembered the blowjob that the Company Commander had given you, and the wonderful climax he had caused. 'Maybe??? Maybe it's not the Saltpeter at all. Maybe we're all just too damned sore and too damned tired to get it up, get it in, get it off, and get it out. Out of a hand or *some* kind of hole. Sounded like the duties of a Marine, though. Maybe.'

One day, you'd led a twenty-five mile march with full gear and backpack, in double-time, no less... at least at the start, stopping only for water breaks, lunch break, and the much needed piss breaks. Quite a few men ended the march with urine stains down the legs of their pants. Thank God for the camouflage-patterned material of their pants. Several men had fallen by the wayside from exhaustion, and RCPO Peabody had called for ambulance and medics on his walkie-talkie as the rest of the Company lumbered on, slower and more out-of-step with each other as the miles mounted.

That night, just as you were dozing off, you were jerked back to full awareness when you heard the moans and groans of *someone* — you only heard one voice — having sex... or what sounded like sex, well, masturbatory sex, anyway. The voice was accompanied by the squishy slap, slap, slap sound of hand-flesh on groin-flesh. Once you'd done it yourself years ago, you recognized the sound anywhere and anytime it occurred.

You could visualize what was going on, or, better yet, coming off, but where, you had no idea; the sounds were coming from everywhere and nowhere in particular. You felt a stirring in your skivvies. You quietly slipped your hand under the blanket and under the sheet; you tweaked your pert nipples and continued down to your rippled, hairless chest and abs, and down underneath the elastic band of your baggy boxers. Limp little Omar was growing and you began stroking in tandem with the sounds bouncing around the stillness and quietness of the night. The usual snoring sounds had stopped, but here and there the squeak of bunk-bed springs began to grow louder and faster. Louder and faster. More slapping noises. More heavy breathing. And then there was a chorus of other moans and groans.

The spokesman for the nighttime self-pleasuring called out, in a none-too-quiet voice, "Loading torpedos, Sir! Loading! Loading! Oh… ohh… Ohhh… OHHHHH! FIRING TORPEDO NUMBER ONE OHHHHH!... FIRING TORPEDO NUMBER TWOOOOO!... FIRING TORPEDO… THREEEEEEE YOWEEEEE OHHHHH GOOOOOD! OWWWWWohhhhh…uhhhhhhhhh." His yells finally transmuted into groans of sexual bliss. And the sounds of the temporary happiness of release and fulfillment.

The lights came on in Chief Jones's quarters; then it filtered through the slats of the Venetian Blinds. The door flew open and he rushed into the dormitory. "WHAT'S GOING ON OUT HERE?" he yelled, the slap of his bare feet resonating on the linoleum floor as he rushed along each of the three aisle ways. "SMELLS LIKE A FUCKIN' WHOREHOUSE, it does!"

There was no answer. In fact, there was no sound but for the ones he, himself, was making, and *those* sounds carried throughout the dorm.

As his footsteps grew louder in the faint moonlight coming through the windows, you opened one eye and saw him, completely naked, his own hairless, floppy penis bouncing from one thigh to the other and back again and again as he hurried past. And it was only then you noticed that, even bare-footed, he moved with that adorable little bouncy walk that had caught your eye the very first day you'd ever seen him. And you smiled. Oh, how you wanted to make love — or was it just — *have sex?* — with that hunk of masculinity, at least once before you graduated from Boot Camp.

And then there was nothing. No sexual sounds. No sounds of flesh beating flesh, nor skin slapping linoleum. His door closed and then his lights turned off. It was then that you heard the sounds of several of the guys taking quick breaths to replenish their depleted lungs.

Disgusted that you'd not fulfilled your craving, you rolled over on your side, hugged the pillow with one arm, and idly wrapped the warm fingers of your other hand around *your* Omar, only to, once again, succumb 'into the arms of Morpheus,' yourself. As Alex would say.

Saturday came and went. Then Sunday morning shown a bright new day. Something was in the air, something unknown, but it brought forth an excited expectation from you. In the Chow Hall at breakfast, you searched people's faces — anyone's face from Okefenokee, or even Atlanta — not that you knew that many people outside the swamp.

'Maybe I shooda gone up ta Waukegan t'day,' you thought to yourself. 'But I ain't knowin' nobody up yonder, 'n' I shore ain't gonna go lookin' fer no floozy jes' so's I kin brag ta tha guys. Don't wanna ketch no dezeeses no way, no how. This way, takin' matters into m'own hands, I kin save me some money and send it down ta Darkness an' his mama 'n' daddy. Help make things a li'l easier fer'em. Ain't sendin' my whorin' mama an' that asshole she's married to, inny money, though.'

You kept looking around as you slowly devoured your three eggs, four pieces of crisp bacon, two patties of very hot and spicy sausage, a slice of half-inch-thick ham, and a huge helping of grits smothered in ham gravy. Oh, yeah… and two heavily buttered buttermilk biscuits and a large glass of real fresh, real cold buttermilk into which you poured a good teaspoon of salt and a tablespoon of black pepper. Nothing like a good li'l ol' Southe'n breakfast for a hungry Southe'n boy. Ummm ummm good!

You tidied-up your place at the table, and carried the tray and dirty tableware to where you were supposed to and headed toward the door leading to the barracks quad. Off to your left side, a figure approached — dark reddish-brown of face, with shiny black hair, and in khaki uniform. Stepping aside, you held back, giving him the courtesy to go first through the hatchway [doorway]. Being yet inside, you nodded and politely acknowledged him with a smile. "Good morning, Petty Officer 1st Class." Your hand motioned toward the door.

He also held back when he nodded and said, "Good morning to you, Seaman Recruit… uhhh… Recruit Leader Petty Officer…" he smiled a big toothy grin and his dark eyes sparkled as he then continued, "...5-Oh-9, isn't it?"

Your eyes flew open in wonderment. You didn't think anyone other than Chief Jones and Company 209 knew your new, but temporary, nickname. But he *did* look familiar.

"You don't remember me, do you, 5-Oh-9?" He chuckled.

"Forgive me, Petty Officer Fir..." you were saying when he interrupted you.

"Let's go outside," he suggested as he motioned toward the door.

"After you, Petty Officer."

"No; after *YOU*, sailor..." You opened your mouth and started to say something, but he pointed straight at you and continued, "...and that's an order!"

"Thank you, Petty Offi..."

Whispering so no one else could hear him, he leaned in and said, "Cut the shit, Pete. It's just you and me. Let's get outside. I got something to tell ya."

You almost saluted, but decided not to when you realized you were still inside. You opened the hatch, stepped through, and led the way down the steps to the sidewalk.

"Where you headed?" he asked.

"No wheres partic'lar."

"That's what I like to hear — your cute Southern drawl. Let's go walk up to the E.M. Club. Okay by you?"

"E.M. Club, Petty Off...?"

"Enlisted Men's Club."

"Oh. Okay," you nodded.

"Wanna shoot a game or two of pool?"

"Never played." You stopped walking, cocked your head, and looked at him with a frown as if to ask, 'Who the hell are you?'

Then he, too, stopped and turned to face you and grinned again. "You still don't remember me, do you?"

"Ya look familyer, but I..."

"I was there, inside the Gate, the day you got off the bus."

Old images flashed through your memory. The frown relaxed, and a faint smile crept across your lips. "Wh... Wa... We..." you struggled aloud to bring his name into your conscious mind.

"Right. Well almost. Davy said you were sharp. It's We'We... We'We Aelred, though most Pale Faces say 'Allred'," he said in a deep, stereotypical Indian way of speaking.

"'Wee-Wee?' That whut people call ya? Ain't it kinda... 'mbarrassin'?"

"Old Injun name," he continued in his heavy baritone voice. "Not 'Wee-Wee', but more like 'Way-Way', and 'Aelred' is more like 'Ail-red'... like in '*ail*ment', but then, Pale Face say this Red Man be '*pain* in ass'." Then he broke into laughter.

So did you. When you calmed down a bit, you said, "I think I'ma gonna like you." Your laughter continued, but in a softer volume... more like a few chuckles.

That, alone, made We'We break into laughter.

By then, you both had resumed your way to the E.M. Club. At your comment about going to like him, We'We had looked toward you, raised an eyebrow for a bit, and then wriggled his brow a few times. You started turning red, yourself.

"While we're out here, alone, I've got a message for you, Pete."

"Frum who?"

"Davy."

"Davy?" you repeated the name. After a couple of seconds, it came to you. "Ya talkin' 'bout Chief Jones?" It had been several weeks since he'd told you to call him 'Davy' or 'D.J.' in private. You'd almost forgotten about that.

"He asked me to tell you to come to his quarters *again* a few minutes before Lights Out *tonight*."

At his saying '*again*', you turned your head to study him.

He looked back at you with a crooked smile and started nodding his head. "Yeah," he said, "I know about the other time you were there after Lights Out." Instantly, you blushed again, turned your head away, and looked down at the ground. "It's all right, Pete," he said, clasping your shoulder and giving a gentle, friendly squeeze. I'm 'family', too. Just wish I could be there tonight, but Davy said you're not ready for that, yet."

You jerked your head back to him. "Not ready fer whut?" you asked rather gruffly.

"I don't know; that's between you guys. I'm just the messenger boy," he sorta teased.

"Holy Jehoshaphat!" you said with a worried tone. "Hope I ain't in inny trouble."

"You? No way!" he exclaimed, shaking his head. "You're the 'Golden Boy' in 209, in Davy's eyes at least. He said he's never met a recru... Awww, shit! I shouldn't be tellin' you this stuff."

"Why not? If it's 'bout me..." you began, but he cut you off.

"That's for him to tell ya; not me. Knowin' him the way I do, I know he'll tell ya in his own good time. Just remember this..." He stopped walking, thereby making you stop, also. His hand, still on your shoulder, squeezed once more. "...He really likes you, Pete, and he's gonna do everything in his power to help you succeed while you're in the Navy."

Then he let his hand drop, you both turned and continued on, soon turning off the sidewalk to the walkway leading up to the E.M. Club. "And if I hear tell of you tellin' him what I just told you..." he glared at you with a mock evil Shaman's stare and, from the deepest part of his throat, growled like a wild animal, "...your ass is gonna be ripped to shreds!"

It wasn't his words that bothered you so much, as was the sudden appearance of the face of a snarling Gray Wolf superimposed over his own face.

You jumped back from the sudden apparition, and then the illusion quickly faded and vanished. We'We grinned an all-knowing smirk and said, "Let's go inside." His point had been made.

And received.

◇◇◇

The time: 2121 hours [that's 9:21 p.m.], nine minutes before Lights Out... Sunday night... in the recruit barracks.

You'd finished the four S's — Shit, Shave, Shower, and Shampoo — and had just slipped into fresh, clean, ecru-colored skivvies — the yellowish-gray-brown didn't show cum- or piss-stains as clearly as white cotton did, and it was close to the color of Caucasian flesh — good for camouflage when push came to shove.

Barefoot and shirtless, you and your newly molded, muscular body approached the windowed wall with closed Venetian Blinds and the closed door leading to the Company Commander's private quarters. Once again, you gave the double-double knock: (knock-knock... knock-knock) And once more you heard the mumbled word, "Enter."

You turned the knob, gently opened the door about a third of the way, stepped in and looked around, finding Chief again sitting at his desk, apparently, once more, wearing nothing but... Whoa! Were your eyes deceiving you?... wearing nothing but an athletic supporter; a jockstrap!

"Close the door," he ordered, but only loud enough *not* to be carried out into the dormitory. When the door clicked shut, he swiveled the chair around, and with exaggerated lip and tongue movement, silently mouthed, "Lock it," as his hand pantomimed turning the deadbolt.

Your eyes perved for the eternity of a second when you looked down at his wide-spread legs, and your vision was quickly drawn to the one exposed testicle protruding out the left side of his pouch. The moist, fleshy bullet and about two inches of his throbbing erection were thrusting above the waistband toward his inny bellybutton.

Slowly... ever so slowly... you licked your lips and, feeling a dribble from the right corner of your lips, you suddenly realized that your mouth was nearly filled with rather thick, viscid saliva, which you gulped down in haste as you turned the lock.

When you went to turn to face him again, you felt his arms wrap around your naked chest, the fingers of his crossed forearms flicking, stimulating the nubbins of your nipples, until they stuck straight out, hot and firm, about half-an-inch. The hardness within his pouch was crushed between your skivvies-covered asscheeks.

He squeezed your arms tighter and lifted you no more than two or three inches off the floor when he whispered in your ear, "Put your heels on top of my feet."

Quickly you obeyed the order, and together, you and he walked back to his small, private bedroom. The last time you'd been in his quarters, you'd been chest to chest, your toes and the balls of your feet were on top of his.

"I want you, Pete. I need you. I've got several things to tell you, but I need this first," his warm... no, *hot*... breath carried the whisper into the innermost depths of your ear. His spit-dripping tongue, rolled into a spear, plunged into your aural opening as far as it possibly could.

And Omar, big, strong, eager Omar, galloped out the slightly opened barn door of your own skivvies, slobbering a long shiny dribble of drool nearly to the hardwood floor, its single eye searching this way and that, up and down, for something soft and warm and moist to kiss. You were primed and ready.

Davy's hands slid seductively across your tits again and only stopped when they were securely placed in your armpits. Effortlessly, he picked you up and threw you across the bed, the rough, woolen blanket and top sheet having already been pulled back and dropped to the floor. He leaned over and once more, his fingers rushed to your pits and delicately slithered down your sides as he softly ordered, "Lift your hips."

Taking no thought, you automatically raised them. His fingers gripped the waistband and yanked them off you. He tossed your shorts — who knows where — again.

Then, slowly, tenderly, he kissed each of your asscheeks, and completely bathed them with his tongue. For a moment or two, his hand then rubbed, massaged, and squeezed your delicious glutes, and you began to feel his heavy, warm breath in the crevice between those perfect cheeks. Not only that, but you could *hear* his sharp, hungry inhalations as the tip of his nose slid millimeter by millimeter deeper, back and forth, up and down along the full length of that tantalizing, inviting cleft, which leads to the Gate of Nirvana's bliss.

Breathing heavy, and with hands nervously gripping the bottom sheet, you looked back, over your shoulder, at the man who was about to break down all your barriers. "Daaaaaaavy," you begged aloud and with pleading eyes, "I know whutcha want… but I'm jes'… not…" You couldn't finish your rejection as you buried your face into the sheet.

Immediately he stopped his ministrations, raised up, and lay down beside you. With one arm bent under his head, his other arm stretched across your back, he started rubbing your other side. "You've never…" he began.

You lifted and turned your face toward his. "No."

"No one?"

"No. Nobody."

"Come'ere," he said, urging you with his arm across your back to slide your naked body closer to his. When your skin touched his, you realized that he, too, was completely naked; somewhere along the way, he had lost the jockstrap. "I won't force you to do anything you don't want to, Pete. I promised you that, and I mean it, no matter how much I want it."

"Thanks," you said, as you squiggled as close to him as possible. Then, tentatively but with an unquenchable desire, you leaned your head toward his and lightly kissed him, not moving your head away from him. In fact, you put your free hand behind his head and pulled it — if possible — closer to you.

His lips opened and you felt the tip of his hot, moist tongue seeking entrance between your own. You let him in and your lips opened wider. Then began the sensual battle to see who could tickle the tonsils of the other, who could claim more of the other's spittle for himself. And it was then you became aware that 'Omar' and 'Little Jonesie' were doing a serpentine mating dance of their own, smearing their thick, sticky sweet nectar over each other.

"We're wasting it," Davy murmured when his tongue retreated. You eased the hold on the back of his head, and he eased back an inch or two, daunting the erotic advances of your tongue. "I want it, Pete. I need it. I've got to have it," he said as he moved down and completely gobbled Omar to the root in a single, unrestrained movement. A single gurgling retch, and then he relaxed his throat, and Omar went deeper — not much, but only as far past his gag reflex as your length would allow. It was then that your tiny lips spit a drop of your pre-seminal fluid into his esophagus.

Up and down, in and out. Up and down, in and out, his mouth and lips slid, sending you higher and higher into sexual ecstasy. You were panting, moaning, squirming, twisting, thrusting.

"Turn around, Davy," he heard you say. "I want it, too. I wanna *try* ta make ya feel as good as you're makin' me." Your breathing was fast. Your breathing was heavy. He knew you were close to the edge, and he pulled off Omar, moving back around to kiss you again. It was long. And passionate. And loving.

As if on cue, you both broke apart and gazed into each other's eyes. "Davy…" you said, wiping the spit off your lips, "… I think… I think I…"

Quickly, he placed two fingers over your lips, preventing you from completing what you were going to say. "Shhhhhhh," accompanied those fingers. "No you don't," he said. "You love what I'm doing, but it's not me that you love. It can't be. Not here. Not as long as we're both here at Great Lakes," he said. Without saying anything, he rubbed the back of his hand over your freshly shaved cheek and around your chin and across your lips. "But we can still enjoy each other from time to time as long as you're here."

Not accustomed to speaking back to adults or to authority figures, you didn't voice an argument, Pete. You accepted what he said as fact. Of course, he knew more about life than you… *AND* he was your superior officer.

You both had gone soft. You reached over and fondled his flaccid cock. He smiled. "You really want to?" he asked as he flexed his growing tumescence in your stroking hand.

You merely nodded your head as you leaned over and barely let Little Jonesie touch your lips. He smelled like clean, fresh soap. You drew back, mentally taking note of every curve, every wrinkle of skin, every variation in color. A clear liquid pearl oozed from his tiny lips. There was no offensive odor, no fruity fragrance, no sickeningly sweet scent. Tentatively, you licked it from its source and found it to be sweet as... as... as... *'YES'*... as sweet as the clear Karo syrup you used on flapjacks back home — the few times you'd had'em — and you shore did like that! It even looked like it! You wanted more. "Ummmmm," you moaned in delight, "it's so good," you said as you pulled away for a brief moment before plunging back down, greedily hungry for that sweet all-night sucker.

"OUCH!" Davy exclaimed. "Don't use your teeth!"

You backed off again and apologized, "Sorry. I didn't think about..."

"That's okay; just *try* to wrap your lips over the edges of your teeth, and don't be so eager. Just take it slow."

You did as he instructed, slowly taking in half-an-inch before drawing back. Then an inch in and back out. Two inches in, and back. And then, at about three-and-a-half inches, Little Jonesie slid against the soft palate at the top of the back of your mouth, and you gagged and quickly withdrew, coughing and hacking-up acidic viscid gunk.

After your short coughing spell ended, Davy said, "Don't try to take more than you're comfortable with, Pete." He slapped you on the back a few times. "It felt fantastic when you were just taking the head in..." he said, "...and running your tongue around the rim. Just take it easy. Now come here."

You stretched out together and hugged and kissed and groped each other until the "little guys" were eager to get busy doing what they did best.

Davy licked your lips, chin, Adam's apple, across both collarbones, and squirmed down farther to kiss, lick, and nibble first one nipple and then the other. You pushed your chest higher, hoping he'd use more pressure. Then, his tongue rushed down your breastbone, across your rippled abs, curled into a spear-point and attacked the remnants of your umbilical scar. The spearing and licking and sucking and even the spit-wet slobbering noises he was making were driving you crazy.

AND OMAR! Omar was spitting-mad, he was! Like a snake, he was weaving, jumping around all over the place, leaving along the way a web of gelatinous pearls and strings of his sweet, yet salty gifts of oral delight. A contraction of your holding-back sent Omar right up next to Davy's fleshy spear of a tongue, and he dribbled a goodly quantity of his honey'd sweetmeat there.

Davy's tongue left the frothy secretion of spittle in the pit of your bellybutton and licked your deliciously moist glans. Up and down and around, his tongue and lips roamed. Inside that delicious hood of extra skin and around the glans the other way, and down and up again, he licked and swiped and flicked and teased.

And you! You twisted and wiggled and thrust with eagerness and dived and licked and sucked and sank down to the root of his hard yet soft, firm yet pliant pleasure-shaft.

Together, you thrust your hips as one; together you mouthed and devoured as much of each other as you could comfortably manage. One hand wrapped around the base of the other's magic flute; the other hand rubbed, massaged, and ever so lightly squeezed the royal family orbs that simultaneously were rushing into hiding ready to spill their seed of life. Nearer and nearer you could tell the time, the moment, the scintillating seconds of eternity were cumming.

You both moaned. You both wanted to warn the other of the cumming explosions, but the adored sensations were too tantalizing; for a brief moment, you both were greedy and thankful for what was about to be received — and given. You could feel it. You could sense it. In the sensual, time-altering moment of forever, you desired for the other, pleasure in the giving and in the receiving of yourselves to each other, and you poured out those feelings to each other, not only physically, but also mentally and emotionally. Spurt after spurt after spurt — who knows how many from either of you, and for that matter, who cares? — it was wonderful, it was satisfying, it was fulfilling, and somewhere, an angel was gaily singing — "It's delightful, it's delicious, it's delectable, it's delirious, it's dilemma, it's delimit, it's deluxe, it's de-lovely". [From: *It's de-Lovely* By Cole Porter, 1936, for the Broadway Musical, *Red, Hot, and Blue*.]

You, Pete, had sucked your first cock — and thoroughly enjoyed it. Whew! 'What's next, and WHEN?' you wondered, both with excitement and trepidation.

CHAPTER EIGHT

Schlomo Fuckatelli-Schmuckatelli

The following morning, Monday, you were tickled pink as you excitedly awoke before Reveille at the usual 0430 hours. Why? Because Chief Jones had told you not more than four hours earlier that after leading the Company on a five-mile wake-up march, you were to lead them to the Chow Hall for breakfast, followed by an hour of calisthenics on the barracks quad, and then an hour and a half at the hospital's pool.

RCPO Alex Peabody would then take the Company from there to Rifle Practice, lunch, and afternoon classes that Jones would help you make-up. And finally, to your great surprise, he told you to meet with Petty Officer 1st Class — now I swear to God… cross my heart and hope to die, I cannot tell a lie; this was his real name — Schlomo Schmuckatelli… at the Quartermaster's shack behind the Hospital at 1530 hours [3:30 pm]. He was the Drill Master of the USNTC Ceremonial Guardsmen. They had talked, and Schmuckatelli was willing to consider taking you on as a member of the Drill Team.

For you, the morning and early afternoon hours dragged on and on. Bored by the every-day routine, but excited by the anticipation of the meeting, the little bounce in Chief Jones's walk became evident in your own.

At the pool, you and Peabody — along with all the other eighty-one naked, hairless recruits — dived in and swam your required number of laps for the day. Your timed results were better than they'd ever been. Peabody finished his final lap-and-a-half behind you, and then joined you as you each took a seat in one of the few deck chairs lined up for visiting observers.

"What's with the spring in your step, 5-Oh-9?" Alex asked. He knew bloody well what was on your agenda for the afternoon and was also aware of your excitement about the prospects.

"Whut 'spring in my step'?" you replied cocking your head to one side as you gave a few wiggles of your hips before you realized what you were doing.

"You're walking the same way Jones does, or didn't you know?" he asked, but before you could answer, he continued, "Maybe it's those late night visits you two have been having. Maybe part of his... *IN-fluence...* has gotten... *IN-side* you. Huhhh?" He grinned as only a Smart Alex could. Oh! that's 'Smart Alec', isn't it?" Heeheehee.

You blushed. You had your own suspicions about Alex's late night disappearances as well. "I don't know *whut* you're talkin' 'bout," you quietly said with such innocence as you both continued watching the guys in the pool.

Then you leaned over toward Alex. Your bare shoulder touched his and you tilted the side of your head toward his and said just above a teasingly serious whisper, "I think... you slimy pollywog... that if the truth be known, we both have the same interest in the Company Commander's quarters, or *something* like that."

He yanked back and jerked his head around glaring at you, and you turned to face him. Both of you fought NOT to burst out laughing. Never mind the perhaps correct *suggested* accusation, 'slimy pollywog' sounded totally alien for a good ol' country boy like you to be using. In your reading, though, you'd recently learned that it was a derogatory piece of Navy slang referring to any sailor of ANY rank, who had NOT crossed the Equator. You looked back at the naked, hairless guys standing around the edges of the pool, and at the butts rising above and sinking back into the water.

(Sigh!)

The clock on the wall indicated it was 1500 hours, thirty minutes before your appointment with Schmuckatelli.

"What are you doing, calling me a 'slimy pollywog?" Alex *almost* yelled.

"Next time you see Chief Jones, ask him if'n he has a Bosun's Punch [3], and you'll find tha answer thar. If he don't, then keep askin' any Chief till ya git one. I'ma goin' to tha rain locker [4]. See ya later."

My, my, my! You sure had been reading up on your Navy Slang [5], hadn't you, 5-Oh-9?

And with that... up, up, and away... and you were gone.

By not leaving USNTC for any Liberties, and by staying nearly 24/7 with Company 209 and your *delightful* Company Commander Jones, you had very little exposure to anyone else, military or civilian.

From the very first moment you and the other newbie recruits stepped off the buses just inside the main gate, you quickly learned that life wasn't a bed of roses away from mama's bosom or your step-daddy's coattails. You were yelled at, cursed at, called all kinds of vile and filthy names — some you'd never heard of, before; you'd been threatened with and/or given the shittiest details, such as scrubbing, naked, on hands and knees, the inside and outside of the toilets and urinals *with your own* toothbrush! It then wasn't long before one of two things happened. (1): You and/or the authorities determined that you were not physically, mentally, or emotionally capable of following orders under pressure, duress, or the generally expected and accepted belittlement of Basic Training, thereby terminating your enlistment with the military. Or (2): You came to realize what was *really* happening. They were building you up and toughening you up on every level; they were teaching you to think for yourself, but also teaching you to follow orders *instantly* (as is needed and duly expected in times of war); and they were teaching you to respect your superiors, each other, and finally, yes, yourself. Too, you realized they were teaching you to keep your head when everything around you seemed in turmoil.

Those things being considered, you found many nights when you were too damned tired to do anything else, much less jerk off, even if they *weren't* lacing your food with that accurse'ed Saltpeter. You'd get in your rack, pull the sheet up, close your eyes, say to yourself the obligatory 'Now I lay me down to sleep…' that you'd habitually done by rote for so many years. When that was finished, and just before you fell asleep, you mentally went over the words of Rudyard Kipling's *If* that you'd learned in the tenth grade.

If you can keep your head when all about you
Are losing theirs and blaming it on you,
If you can trust yourself when all men doubt you
But make allowance for their doubting too,
If you can wait and not be tired by waiting,
Or being lied about, don't deal in lies,
Or being hated, don't give way to hating,
And yet don't look too good, nor talk too wise:

If you can dream–and not make dreams your master,
If you can think–and not make thoughts your aim;
If you can meet with Triumph and Disaster
And treat those two impostors just the same;
If you can bear to hear the truth you've spoken
Twisted by knaves to make a trap for fools,
Or watch the things you gave your life to, broken,
And stoop and build 'em up with worn-out tools:

If you can make one heap of all your winnings
And risk it all on one turn of pitch-and-toss,
And lose, and start again at your beginnings
And never breath a word about your loss;
If you can force your heart and nerve and sinew
To serve your turn long after they are gone,
And so hold on when there is nothing in you
Except the Will which says to them: "Hold on!"

If you can talk with crowds and keep your virtue,
Or walk with kings–nor lose the common touch,
If neither foes nor loving friends can hurt you;
If all men count with you, but none too much,
If you can fill the unforgiving minute

With sixty seconds' worth of distance run,
Yours is the Earth and everything that's in it,
And–which is more–you'll be a Man, my son!

The tranquil sense of quietude and peace inspired by those words would lull you into a blissful sleep, and the next morning, you'd awaken refreshed, only to be met head-on with more of the same... ol'... shit.

You left the Hospital by the rear entrance, crossed the delivery road, and went around the Quonset hut to the front entrance. The sign over the door read, 'Quartermaster'. Entering, you removed your white cap, and looking around, spotted a Yeoman Second Class sitting at a desk. You had just turned eighteen when you enlisted; he couldn't be much older — maybe nineteen, or twenty at the most. Nice body, as his smartly tailored uniform hugged the muscles; mousy-brown hair, still short — more like the Marines' 'high & tight' cut; and lips that were full and red and moist.

"You look lost," he said, turning from the ledger book in which he'd been writing. [Remember, this was fifty-some years ago — they didn't have computers.] "Can I help you?"

"Good afternoon, Yeoman." Recognizing the Insignia he wore, you'd given the mandatory greeting of enlisted personnel while at Recruit Training Center Great Lakes, as you neared the desk.

"Good afternoon, '*Re-crew-it*'," he responded with the customary and derogatory pronunciation given to all newbies. He recognized you by your haircut and shaved arms, exposed by your short-sleeved work shirt.

You snapped to and sang out, "Seaman Recruit Dix reportin' as ordered for appointment at 1530 hours with Petty Officer First Class Sssssuck... Smuck... Schmuck... SCHMUCKATELLI, Sir... uhhh... Yeoman." Boy! Were *you* embarrassed by fuckin' up the name!

The Yeoman tried to hold back, but you could see him struggling with a quiet snicker. Then with a loud snort, a gob of nasal booger-juice flew out and splatted over the ledger page. "FUCK!" he exclaimed, shaking his hand as he pointed down the passageway to his left (your right). "Last door on the right," he roared.

"Thank ya, Yeoman," you said, grinning, as you turned, proceeded a couple of steps, and chuckled to yourself, which he must have heard.

It was then you heard the wooden legs of a chair scrape the marble-like terrazzo floor, followed by what sounded like a fist hitting a desk as he yelled. "Get your ass back here, you fuckin' NUB [6]," he yelled as he stood up and pointed to the floor on the front side of the desk.

Quickly, you hundred-and-eightied and returned to where he indicated. "Yes, Yeoman?" You looked scared as a chicken 'bout ta git its head chopped off.

He slowly pointed to the gob of snot. In a superior, calm voice, he ordered, "Lick it up."

You looked down at it, then up into his baby blues. "Sir?" you respectfully asked, not believing what you'd just heard.

"RE-CREW-IT!" he scorned. "I told you to lick it up... or do I have to send you to Sick Bay to get a hearing aid?" His complexion had turned livid red; his voice sounded angry.

'Obedience is better than valor,' you heard Davy's voice in your head. Without another word, you slowly leaned forward, your tongue already sticking out of your mouth; your stomach was spasming toward vomit. But about halfway to the ledger book you stopped. Others of Chief Jones's own words were flying around inside your memory banks. You straightened up, stood tall, looked the Yeoman square-on and with all the politeness you knew, you said, "Yeoman... you can bust me ta Chief Jones if you like, but I'm not doin' it! Not that!"

His color gradually returned to normal. He stared at you with no expression except for the tiny grin that was beginning to grow across his face. He extended his right hand in... *friendship*???

"Good going, Dix. Not many recruits know when to draw the line and say, 'No'. You're learning fast."

You relaxed a little, reached out, and shook his offered hand, as he continued.

"How long have you been in?"

"This is my seventh week; five more to go."

"Well, good luck to ya. Study hard, do what you're told… *usually!*" he grinned and chuckled, "and continue to keep your head on straight. You're nobody's fuck-toy; it may seem like it at times, but you're not." Then his tone changed and he pointed to the boogered ledger page and ordered, "Now… wipe it up… with your *fingers*," he emphasized.

You just looked at him and then cocked your head to the side like a puppy dog who doesn't understand his Master's words. In all your innocence, you didn't know HOW he could order you or anyone else to do such a foul thing.

"You heard me. I told you to wipe it up with your fingers. NOW DO IT!"

Glancing quickly down at the damp smudge, your eyes returned to his as you placed your white cap on the left corner of the desk. Then, you joined your index and middle fingers of your right hand and swiped across the mess. You turned your hand palm-up so that he could see that you had done as he ordered. And you shivered with revulsion.

He looked down. "You missed some." He looked into your eyes. "Use your other hand and get the rest of it."

You acquiesced and did as he ordered. As you straightened up and showed him both upturned hands, he said, "Come around here," he indicated directly in front of him as he turned facing toward the passageway leading to Schmuckatelli's office.

You moved around the end of the desk to stand where you thought he had pointed, your hands still facing upward.

"Closer," he demanded, "and then stand still."

One step forward and you brought your other foot up to and against the first. You two were only about a foot apart. He exhaled a huge breath directly into your face; you smelled the stale odor of cigarettes, turned your head, and restrained a cough. "You took your damn good time, Dix. I expect Recruits to hop to and be faster when ordered to do something; think you can do that?" he asked.

You opened your mouth to answer, but he held up his hand as a stop sign. "Don't reply… and remember to stand still!"

He reached toward your tan webbed belt, slid the bar from its locking position, and released the webbing from the brass buckle entirely. He then undid the waist button of your work pants, unzipped the zipper, and yanked the flaps of the pants to either side, exposing your tannish skivvies. "Now wipe my gooey snot on your shorts…"

He paused long enough for you to do so, and you did, several times, until your fingers no longer felt slimy or clammy."

"…secure the zipper…" You did. "…secure the belt…" You did, and he pointed down the passageway once again. "Now go to your appointment. You're already late," he said with a mischievous all-knowing look in his eye.

You turned and once again headed down the passageway.

You hadn't taken more than three hurried steps, and he called after you, "Still want your cap?"

"Awww, shit!" you said louder than a whisper but softer than normal. You stumbled while turning, but righted yourself as you scurried back. "Sorry, Yeoman," you said, grabbing the cap, and again turning, more carefully that time.

"Good luck with Fuckatel… SCHMUCKatelli," he corrected himself; "you'll need it." He laughed… presumably at his own faux pas.

You dared not make a sound, but you waved your cap in the air as you rushed down the passageway to the last door on the right. A hand-made sign hung from a thumbtack: "ENTER AT YOUR OWN PERIL".

'What the hell?' you asked yourself. You gave your usual double-double knock. <knock-knock… knock-knock>

"Door's open; can't you read the sign?" a deep, gruff voice growled from within.

With a bit of caution, you slowly opened the door and timidly entered. The room was a total mess. Clutter everywhere. Papers and books strewn about helter-skelter. Wastebaskets overflowing. And the stench was abominable — like a rank unattended, smoky, pissy, cummy shit-house on the far edge of an older, unkempt city park — you know the kind I'm talking about. No doubt a pungent, stiff, old cum-rag or two was standing about somewhere in all the trash.

And then there was the raunchy, disheveled, unshaven old "Salt" sitting behind what would ordinarily be considered a desk. He looked to be at least... well... way beyond the age of retirement.

Standing up straight, you announced, "Seaman Recruit Di..."

"You're seven minutes late... 5-OH-9! That's one strike against you," he said without looking up from what he was writing. "I won't stand for that, not one fuckin' minute. By the way, how's your peter hangin', Dix? Jones told me all about you." And then he guffawed himself into a hacking cough of a cigarette fit.

You quickly shuffled around the desk and began slapping the old man on his back.

"No! Never touch the Drillmaster," he pulled away with a husky, raspy, wheezing voice. Get back over there," he indicated in front of the desk.

Eventually, you were where he wanted you, and his coughing ceased for the time being. "This won't take long," he said.

"Petty Offic..." you began, but he cut you off.

"Not a word outta ya," he ordered. "Listen to me. You'll have your time to talk."

Folding your white cap, you draped it over the top of your pants — half inside, half out. You stood at Attention, listening to every word.

"You probably want to be in the Drill Team because you're not cut out for all the PT [Physical Training], and you want to *perform* in the snazzy uniform; you're a pretty one, you are. You'd look good out there; that's for sure."

You couldn't tell if he was thinking out loud, perving on you, or stating what he *might* consider obvious. Schmuckatelli DID seem to lick his lips when a pause came between his words, though. But he went on with his speech.

"You're coming into Drill Training late; if you really wanted it, you shoulda signed up for it when you enlisted. I only need twenty-four full-timers. I've got those — they're VERY good — and I've got five extras who're stand-ins or replacements for the rare member who gets wounded, or *worse*, from the razor-sharp bayonets. It's not a game, being in the Drill Team, sailor; it's serious, dangerous work. Even life-threatening!"

You took a deep breath and glanced down at the litter on the floor.

"You're having second thoughts, now, aren't you, kid? Don't answer; I know you are."

You looked up at him.

"And if you become a member of the Drill Team, there's not a helluva lot you can advance to. Your pay grade will basically remain the same for however long you're here." He paused for a minute, thinking, eyeballing you from head to toe. He held out his hand and drew a circle in the air with his finger pointing down, silently telling you to turn around. When your back was to him, he said, "STOP!" and then he added, "Pull your pants tight across your butt."

You were feeling *very* uncomfortable with Petty Officer First Class Schmuckatelli, but you did as he ordered.

More to himself than to you, he commented, "Nice. Very nice." Then, pointedly, he said, "Continue turning around."

When you again faced him, he said, "Stop; that's enough. Now... pull your pants tight across your hips."

When you did, he scrunched up his mouth to one side. "Hmmmmmmmm," you heard coming from his throat as he nervously tapped the desk with his fingertips. His reactions didn't make you any more hopeful. Or relaxed. "By the looks of things, you might have to wear a jock strap during maneuvers. I don't want your balls to get in the way, or a hard-on to give you any queer distraction. Drop your pants and your skivvies," he flatly ordered.

"WHAT?... uhhh... Sir?... uhhh... Petty Off..."

"That's strike two. JUST DO IT, re-crew-it! HOP TO IT! I don't have all fuckin' day." He pointed to the floor around you again.

You took too long in releasing the brass buckle of your belt.

"Too long. Orders are given and meant to be carried out immediately. Strike three. Six weeks lost with no practice. Strike four. I only allow two. You're out. Good afternoon, re-crew-it. I'll make my report to Jones. Close the door behind you."

He rose from the chair behind the desk, scratched his balls through the crotch of his pants (they were probably stuck to his legs with dried cum), turned, and looked out the window at the Drill Team practicing on the quad across the street. They were flipping their pieces to one another. [If you don't understand what that *really* means, ask a sailor; there's a *double entendre* in nearly everything they say.]

'That dirty old disgruntled pervert.'

And make his report to CPO Jones, Drillmaster Fuckatelli certainly did, quicker than you could have told him to bend over and spread'em.

You didn't even think of joining the rest of the Company for the last class of the day — a class on Seamanship — you just walked back to the barracks, sulking, due to the disappointing events that had, only moments before, taken place.

Not meaning to be sneaky or secretive, you quietly entered the dormitory and headed to your rack.

Jones's door was open and a lively WWII tune was playing on the radio. You thought it was so very gung-ho that CPO Jones was listening to music that was popular while he was probably aboard ship during the war, but you'd never talked about it. The song on the radio was Hoagy Carmichael's *Billy-A-Dick*.

> *Every night while I'm undressin',*
> *sayin' my prayers and lightly confessin',*
> *I can hear hot licks*
> *from a set of drums upstairs.*

Well, it couldn't be Johnny 'cause he isn't there;
Johnny's overseas. We know not where.
But, believe it or not, every night on the dot
I can hear a tenor drum say:

Billy-a-dick, Billy-a-dick, tick, tack.
When's that character comin' back?
When's that kid in the G.I. lid
gonna choo-choo down the track?

By the time you walked down the center aisle, you noticed through the partially closed Venetian Blinds that that he was sitting there on his daybed, naked, with his eyes closed, beatin' his meat to the rhythm of the song. You watched through the slats.

Poor ol' me, I'm beat as can be,
and my rim has even started to rust.
Look at these sticks tryin' to take out the licks,
they're covered with an inch of dust, beep-a-dust.

Billy-a-dick, Billy-a-dick, tick, tack.
When's that character comin' back?
When's that boy with the jumpin' joy
gonna launch that last attack?

Did you dare? 'Nuthin' could be better rite now,' you thought as you tiptoed silently through the door, closed it and locked it, and pulled the cords on the Blinds, closing them to all unwanted eyes. Without removing your clothes, you carefully stepped over to the bed and between his spread knees. Carefully you knelt down and then leaned in and devoured the slick, moist head of his dick.

His eyes flew open and he yanked your head away. Discovering it was you, he looked around and saw that you'd secured the door and blinds.

"You scared the fuckin' shit outta me, but don't stop now. I'm so close," he said, then shoved your mouth back down on his still-throbbing dick. The music continued.

If he'll roll, roll, roll like a drumstick;
Chewin', chewin', chewin' on a gumstick.

Jack, we'll soon have a dark-eyed derby
and beat it like a cymbal on a music rack.

And on the word 'cymbal', your mouth and throat were filled with his bitter-sweet baby-makers. From what you'd heard since you enlisted, you guessed that he'd either been drinking Scotch, or eating asparagus. 'Nuf said. But bitter or sweet, you loved it. Because it was his.

However, your rejection by Fuckatelli-Schmukatelli showed through your pleasuring of Jones. Sure, you went through the motions with apparent ease and desire, but your body refused to allow for your own firm excitement.

He flopped down on his back from his sitting position and said, "Come here, sailor." You turned to sit on the bed beside him, but that's not what he wanted. "Not that way, but this..." he patted his chest with one hand as he pulled you down on top of him with the other.

Your shirted chest was against his naked, hairless one; your right hip was on the bed, and everything below was dangling off the side.

"Come on up here, all the way, Pete, and put your legs between mine." You did as he told you to. "Now just relax." He wrapped his arms around your back and pulled you tight. His naked legs wrapped around your butt and your clothed groin pressed against his nakedness. Your chin rested in the crook of his left shoulder, and you breathed in the day-old aroma of masculine sweat. You took a deep breath and let it out slowly. Your clothed body seemed to meld into his soft, warm nudity. For a brief few, quiet moments, you felt more relaxed than you'd ever been since enlisting. Your pulse and your breathing were in counterpoint to his — when he breathed in, you breathed out; when he breathed out, you breathed in. You felt safe, and warm.

"I got a phone call a few minutes ago," he said.

"From Petty Officer Schmuckatelli?"

"Yeah."

"I guess you know he didn't accept me."

"Yeah, I know. Not much advancement in the Drill Team, anyway, Pete."

"That's what he said."

After a few minutes of relishing the closeness and warmth of each other, he said, "Let's get up so I can get dressed. Everybody'll be back soon."

You guys kissed and separated, then you stayed sitting on the bed while he dressed.

"I know you had your heart set of getting into the Drill Team, but since I got the call from Schlomo, an idea has been running through my head, but I want to ask you a question before I tell you what it is."

His tone sounded military, so you tried to sound military when you said, "All right, Chief."

After the essentials, shirt, pants, and tie were on, he slipped into his shinny, black, lace-up shoes. Hiking his left foot onto the edge of the bed close to your right hip, he asked, "Have you given any thought to any other line of duty you'd like to be assigned to while you're in the Navy"

Oh, I don't know," you said, leaning back on your knees. "There ain't much I know innythang 'bout 'ceptin' huntin' and fishin' and growin' thangs," you thought out loud, slipping back into your drawl as you gazed unseeingly at the floor, your chin cupped in your hands, and your elbows anchored on your knees. "Shore enjoyed teachin' Darkness his letters an' numbers an' the Semaphore Code. An' I learned a lot from Vashti 'bout healin' and helpin' wounded animals… OH YEAH! An' there was tha time when Shadrach had a bellyache right here…" You sat up and pointed to the area between your right hip and your crotch. "…an' she had me helpin' as she cut'im open and removed part o' his gut."

"YOU'RE SHITTIN' ME!"

"Nope. Vashti had some BIGGGGG Voodoo magic… an' the help of a lot of Rum for puttin'im 'sleep and cleanin' tha cut," you said, rubbing your side where his incision would have been. "It looked so purty inside thar… bright reds, yellows, whites… inside that black skin o' his! I couldn't believe it; but I shore did like lookin' inside his body."

While you were describing the scene, Jones stood back, his arms crossed across his chest, his head cocked to the right, and he was either sucking or biting on his lower lip; but it was obvious he was thinking about *something*.

He looked at his wristwatch. "Shit!" he exclaimed. "I forgot about an appointment," he lied. "Open the blinds, turn off the lights, and let's get outta here," he said, picking up his wallet, handkerchief, and car keys. "If I'm not back by chow time, march the guys over to the chow hall; okay?" he asked, then quickly added, "Why am I asking? THAT'S AN ORDER, SAILOR!"

"Aye, aye, Chief!" you, too, had switched instantly back into military mode. He leaned forward and gave you a quick, chaste kiss on the lips, and was gone. You pulled the door closed and watched his ass bounce to those perky steps of his as he rushed farther and farther away, and finally out the door of the barracks.

CHAPTER NINE

Corpsman vs Corpse-man; Hanger Party

Evening chow came and went, with no sign of Chief Jones to be found anywhere around. Alex and you, it seemed, were in charge of the Company. Everyone knew the routine and there were no problems. *Taps* sounded and the lights went out automatically; still, no appearance of the Chief.

Your sleep that night was troubled. You'd doze for a while, then, at the slightest noise, open your eyes and look toward his quarters for any sign of movement. Finally, even in your slumber, you heard the familiar leather-soled steps heading toward his door. A key in the lock, and it opened and closed; his light came on and the Blinds were closed.

All was well, and you rolled over on your other side and fell fast asleep, until *Reveille* was sounded and the lights in the dormitory came on at 0430 hours. Another damn beautiful day of marching, exercises, and classes. <Yawn>

Before you could finish your morning piss, you heard Jones's voice over the P.A. system. "RCPO Peabody and RLPO 5-Oh-9… report to my office, AS YOU ARE, *on* the double."

"Oooooo," mocked several of the guys, some wriggling their foreheads suggestively. One guy slapped you on your skivvies-covered ass as he walked past. At the trough-style urinal, the guy next to you was smiling when he turned to you with his morning hard-on in hand, and stroked it a few times. Or maybe it *wasn't* a morning hard-on, but it looked hard and was long and thick with a drop of something at the tip of his foreskin, not clear and yet not yellow. Oh, well.

You looked perplexed as you shook the last drops and shoved Omar back inside your skivvies.

Peabody was in the middle of shaving with his Gillette Double-Edged razor. Half his face was finished, and the other half still covered with lather. With soap-cup, razor, and washcloth in hand, he angrily shouted, "Fuckin' 'A' ditty-bag! *Now* what?"

"Yeah, *now* what?" you asked as you joined him on the way to Jones's quarters. You both had nothing but towels wrapped around your waists.

The door was open, and Jones was standing there — in uniform — his hands high on either side of the doorjamb. "Good morning, men. Come on in," he greeted you both. Once you were inside, he closed the door. "This won't take long, so you don't need to sit down. "By the way, that's kinda cute, Alex," he said as he used a couple of fingers to wipe some lather from the RCPO's cheek and then proceeded to give him some white hash marks across his forehead and one down the bridge of his nose.

Loosening the corner of the towel, Alex bared his all as he wiped the lather from his face.

"Hurry up and cover yourself; the Blinds are open," Jones told him.

"What's up, Chief?" you and Alex asked simultaneously.

"Thanks for taking over, yesterday, guys. I knew I could count on you."

"Ya had me worried, Davy. I thought somethin' had happened to ya while ya were out on yer appointment, like getting' in a car wreck or... or sumpin'," you said, Petey, openly showing how much you really cared for the Chief, and comfortable enough with it that you slipped back into your drawl. Your eyes glistened, but you held your "unmanly" tears back.

"Well," Jones began, "nothing like that happened; no wreck; no accidents; nothing. The appointment led to another and then another, and finally a fourth one."

You and Alex looked at each other with concern on your faces, silently asking something like, 'Why's he telling us this?'

Answering your unspoken questions, he continued. "This morning, I'll lead the calisthenics and five-mile run. I want you both in formation with the rest of the Company. Then, we'll end the march at the chow hall."

"But why, Chief?" Alex asked,

"Have we done something wrong?" you asked.

He put his right hand on your left shoulder, Pete; remember? And his left hand on Alex's right shoulder, and said, "You guys haven't done anything but what I ordered you to do. I just got my ass chewed for having you do most of my work for me. Guys like you could spoil me," he said with a chuckle and a smile and he affectionately slapped your cheeks — the ones on your faces, not the ones covered by your towels.

"Awww, shucks," you said, blushing.

"Come on, Chief; there's more to it than that. An ass chewing would take no more than a telephone call; or even one appointment. But *four*? Did the others have anything to do with that? Or can you tell us?" That was Alex asking.

"You've got less than three weeks before you graduate from Boot Camp. You've *both* given me more than I could ever ask for..." As the words slipped from his lips he grinned and wriggled his forehead, and added an aside, "...but we won't mention that to anybody."

You and Alex again looked at each other, with surprise at having your suspicions about each other confirmed. An evil grin spread across both your faces. But Jones drew your attention back to himself.

"Alex..." he began, "you'll just be handling most of my paperwork from now until graduation." Then, without any hesitation, he went on. "I'm gonna be honest with you, Alex. Nine weeks ago, when I first met you, I didn't think you'd make it. I thought you were a spoiled rotten little rich kid whose Senator-father could make anything happen to change anything you didn't like, but..." and he quickly and repeatedly pointed to Alex, "... you didn't even call home when I ordered you and the Company to crawl through the mud and under the barbed-wire with live ammo flying overhead. Ya made me proud that day, Alex, and I..."

Unlike his usual manners, Alex interrupted Jones, and asked, "May I say something, Chief?"

He nodded his assent.

"You're right. I *was* a spoiled rotten little rich kid whose Senator-father could make happen what you said. For all of my eighteen years, everyone's been too scared to say 'No' to me and *gave* me everything I wanted, but you made me *earn* every privilege I got. Thank you, Davy. I think I'm on my way to becoming my own man, and with your help, I'll continue."

Jones was beaming. He was also biting his lower lip, probably to keep his emotions from showing through his macho image. "Thank you, babe..."

Suddenly, Jones froze. He'd had a slip of the tongue and feared how you might react, Pete. In fact, he was petrified. As soon as the word was out of his mouth, his expression changed and he jerked his sight to you. "Uhhhhh..." He tried to say something, but the words wouldn't come.

"It's all right. I've known for a while," you said.

"How?" Jones asked.

"When?" Alex asked.

"Welllllll..." you drew the word out, looking more smug than you ever had before, "do you remember that morning when ya gave me a pair o' my own skivvies an' ya tol' me that you'd found 'em back there in the little bedroom? Ya said that Davy went back ta git y'all some coffee, an' ya wuz lookin' 'round an' found 'em under tha edge of the bed..." you pointed back toward the kitchenette and bedroom, "...an' actu'ly stole 'em? Do ya remember tellin' me that, Alex?" you asked with an accusing grin.

The color had drained from his face. He was fidgety. His eyes were jerking back and forth between yours and Jones's.

"Ye... yeah... I..." he mumbled.

"Ya *lied* ta me; didn' ya, *PEA-body*?" you faked your anger, but you were no master at *that*. "I must've taken'em off during my sleep, and you found'em either on my sheet or on the deck, and you pocketed them." You couldn't control the laughter that burst forth; you'd caught him lying. And, *SHIT!* You couldn't even keep the fierce look on your face as the shit-eating grin spread from ear to ear.

"You asshole!" he exclaimed, balling-up his fist and slamming it into your upper arm.

"Ouch! But it serves ya right. Yer expression just now was like a 'coon what's been caught stealin' frum tha cow's feed-bucket." You snorted a repressed chuckle.

"Okay, guys," Jones broke in. "You've had your fun, and we don't have all morning for this shit. Peabody, go finish shaving and get your fatigues on. We'll talk more, but later."

"Right, Chief," he said, leaving. "See ya, guys." He closed the door behind him.

"Now, Pete..." Jones said, "I'm releasing you from your duties as RLPO as of this morning."

"Why, Chief..." you blurted out without thinking of military protocol, "... have I... have I... done somethin' wrong?" Suddenly, the room felt cold, even though it was still summertime and there was no air conditioning running.

"No, no, no, no, no," he quickly tried to reassure you. "Pete..." he paused and cocked his head to one side, squinting his eyes as if he were looking into the very depths of your soul. You dared not say anything until he was finished. "...I've been watching you, but more than that, I've been listening to you... listening to every word you've said when you're around me."

"Yessir."

"You've done a lot of reading, both, when you were in school, and since you enlisted. I've seen how much you enjoy helping other people. And you, yourself, told me how much you enjoyed helping... what's her name? The black woman back home? Vashti?"

You nodded your head.

"... how much you enjoyed helping her when she removed... her husband's appendix. Right?"

"Yeah, Chief, but what's that got to do wi...?"

He held up his finger, silencing you. "I've talked to several people... people in authority... and I've gotten permission for you to miss morning exercises, drills, marches, and all that stuff, but you have to be back here at 1300 hours for chow and afternoon classes with the rest of the Company until you graduate from Basic."

"Back here? From where?" you asked, seemingly confused and with no drawl whatsoever.

Jones smiled for a moment, loving to see you squirm. Then he said, "After this morning's chow, I want you to go over to the main Hospital, and I want you to go up to the Third Floor and ask for Hospital Corpsman Petty Officer 2nd Class Fred Johnson."

"Why? Is sumthin' wrong with me?"

"No. Oh, God, no, Pete. Don't you worry yourself about that. I've gotten special permission — that's what all the meetings were about yesterday afternoon and last night — to move you from Seaman Recruit to Hospitalman Recruit, and after you graduate from Boot Camp in three weeks, you and all other Recruits will be entitled to two weeks Leave, IF you should decide to take it. If not — or when you come back from Leave — you'll become a Hospitalman Apprentice while in Naval Hospital Corpsman School here at Great Lakes. Now, no more..." he started to say, but seeing your expression, asked, "Why so perplexed? You gotta question? Huh?"

Scratching your head, you said, "Chief... you're talkin' 'bout hospitals an' hospitalmen an' coremen... well... honestly, I don't see whut one's gotta do with th'other."

"What do you mean by that?" he asked. "A Hospitalman and a Corpsman are basically the same, and both can work in hospitals."

"A Hospitalman is like a Nurse, isn't he?"

"Can be. Or a Pharmacist's Mate, or a Surgical or other kind of medical Technician, or an Admin Assistant, or a Medic in the Marines, or any number of other positions. Hospital Corpsman is the largest and most decorated rating in the entire Navy."

With total sincerity and a genuine lack of understanding, you said, "But I thought a *coreman* would drill down in the ground and pull up core samples at construction sites for the Seabees."

There was a moment of, shall we say, *shocked...* silence, and then the Chief broke into gales of laughter; that's the only way to describe it. He just went on and on; he couldn't stop, and he wrapped his arms across his gut, it hurt so bad. But, as the old saying goes — all good things must come to an end. Wiping the tears from his face, the laughter ceased.

"I just don't believe you, Pete..." he said as the laughter burst forth again. But it didn't last as long that time.

"You laughing *AT* me, Chief? I guess I'm still nothin' but a clodhopper." You looked so sad when you said that.

"No, no," Jones said, chuckling, as he grabbed you by the shoulders and pulled you into a gigantic bear hug, not caring if anyone saw the scene through the open door or Blinds. "I wasn't laughing at you, Petey. That's one of the things that I love about y..."

You jerked your head back so you could look him in the eyes.

"...one of the things I... *like...* about you so much — your innocence." He released the hug and held you at arms' length. Quick lesson, 5-Oh-9. Then you gotta get dressed, and we gotta go to chow."

"Okay, Chief."

Hearing the coldness in your voice, he tried to reassure you by saying, "Honestly, I wasn't laughing at you, Pete. Come on over to the desk for a minute; I wanna show you something."

A few steps later and he was sitting at his desk and you were standing at his left side.

"There's not a rating that's called a coreman." He wrote 'c-o-r-e-m-a-n' on a piece of paper. "But a Hospital Corpsman..." he said each letter aloud as he wrote, "... is spelled, 'C-o-r-p-s-m-a-n'. The 'P' is silent; you don't pronounce it. 'Corps' is a French word that General George Washington used in 1776 when he founded JAG, the Judge Advocate General's Corps. Everyone in our military from Seamen Recruits and Privates all the way up to the Commanders-in-Chief *SHOULD* know that the word is spelled 'c-o-r-p-s'. Until 1941, the Air Force was known as the Army Air Corps. We've got the Marine Corps, the Signal Corps, the Quartermaster Corps, and in civilian life, we've got the Press Corps."

[*Author's Note:* The Peace Corps didn't come about until President Kennedy's 1961 order to establish it.]

"Oh, my God!" you said. "I feel like such an idiot."

"Good Lord, why?"

"Every time I saw it written out, I said in my head, 'Corpse-man', and I thought a Corpsman worked in the hospital's morgue with all the corpses."

Well, some do... if they specialize in Pathology. Or necrophilia. Now... that's a *real* 'CORPSE-MAN'.

Later that morning and during the next five mornings, you learned your way around the Hospital. You pushed meal carts around to many of the patients; you emptied individual urinals and bed pans; you learned to give enemas; you learned to exercise patients' legs and arms — always under the watchful eye of a Corpsman or a Nurse. It wasn't always pleasant, but you could see and feel the satisfaction of being able to help other guys through some of their pain. And you realized that the more you learned, the more you'd be able to help.

Yes, Jones had been right — having you transferred before the Navy sent you to Gunnery or Mechanics or Construction school. Of course, those areas are absolutely necessary and mandatory, but not all sailors are cut out for the more manual jobs. And in *any* of the Armed Forces, *NONE* of the Specialist jobs are menial; they are *ALL* necessary! And they are all rewarding when you can say to yourself, or have someone else tell you, "Job well done, sailor."

AND — and here's where it gets interesting — you quickly discovered that Jones had sent you in search of Hospital Corpsman Petty Officer 2nd Class Fred Johnson, but what he *didn't* know was that Fred Johnson was already known to you as 'Red' Johnson, from the Atlanta airport and your flight to Chicago nine weeks earlier. Just the very thought of working with your own ivory-skinned, red-headed, freckle-faced, green-eyed fantasy 'Popeye the Sailorman', caused the 'tingle in your dingle' to raise Omar's little oozing head more than once during those first six mornings as a Corpsman Apprentice.

But it didn't stop there.

Johnson had an apartment about three miles south-south-east of USNTC, North Chicago, in the little community of Lake Bluff, just a block from the water's edge of Lake Michigan. It was nothing to write home about, but it was neat and clean and cozy enough for the intimate little party he was beginning to plan for Saturday evening after he learned of your being transferred to his *tutelage*, shall we say? He even got Jones to approve Liberty for you, for *both,* Saturday and Sunday nights; he'd see to it that you'd be back at the base around 0430 Monday morning.

"Oh, really???" Jones had asked Fred/Red. "Something going on here that I should know about?"

"Not yet," Johnson answered with a wink and a grin.

You rode to the party with Jones and — believe it or not — Seaman Recruit Floyd Reginald Alexander Peabody the Third. Already there, were Byron Sweetwater and his 'sidekick', Hank Snow. To your great surprise, Red, Byron, and Hank were completely naked, wearing nothing more than cock-rings and butt-plugs, and you learned that most of Red's little *soirées* were also thought of as 'hanger parties' — you walked in, hung up ALL your clothes, and let everything hang out (as it were), or stand at Attention for the entire evening. Davy had helped you with the cock-ring, but you refused the butt-plug.

Oh, well. All for one; one for all. It just might very well turn out to be a *VERY* fulfilling and interesting weekend. You and Davy and Alex rushed into the bedroom and stripped. Their nakedness wasn't new to you. Neither were Byron's and Hank's, but Red! What a 'Popeye the Sailorman' he was! You saw ripples and muscles you never even imagined on a fellow human being. And he *DID* have that coppery brillo pad of pubic hair that you had imagined that first time you'd met, there in the Atlanna air port.

'But he's not a human,' you thought to yourself. 'He's a god from Mount Olympus!'

He saw drool escape from the corner of your mouth, and he winked at you with a mischievous smile. But just then, the doorbell rang and he went to answer it.

"Who is it?" he called out. Names you recognized were given and, standing back so as not to be seen, he cracked the door open just wide enough for Rollo Burnside and Pacheco Keskeskeck to enter. After quick 'Hello's', Red led them, too, back to the bedroom to shed and hang up their clothes. Soon, two more huggable, kissable, lickable, suckable hunks were in the living room. And everybody was wearing at least a cock-ring, if not a butt-plug. Red and Davy and Hank and Rollo had been cut; you and Alex and Byron and Pacheco all had varying lengths of skin dangling from your dripping cocks, all the way from Alex's very short *partial* covering to Pacheco's inch-and-a-half or more, covering that Portobello-like head — a veritable 'Omnibus' of *smörgåsbord*, all. 'Something for everyone,' to borrow the slogan of the '50s and '60s TV show.

Red had set out a buffet on the small dining-room table. The chairs had been removed and placed along the only bare wall in the L-shaped living/ dining room; that way, someone could be bobbing his head on a throbbing piece of still-attached meat, while the host of that particular piece of meat was nibbling from a plateful of delectable goodies from the table. Such nonchalance for such an intimate gift. But it sure was fun to push the limits.

But the most fun for you was when you were standing close to the table, taking a bit of this and a bit of that, while under the table, *someone* was sampling your own sweet-and-sour sauce, a few drips to this one, a few drops to that one, but you held back your full load/s for later.

There were the usual buffet nibbles — a plate of assorted snack crackers, another of various cuts of rye, pumpernickel, French, and Italian breads, a platter of cold cuts, another of sliced cheeses, the usual condiments, a bowl of mixed nuts, a larger bowl of sweet, colorful fruit salad sprinkled with shredded coconut; raw veggies with several different dips, a large crystal bowl of Champagne Punch, bubbling and overflowing with dry ice fog. And last, but by no means least, was a candle-heated chaffing dish with little bits of dark meat soaking in a mixture of melted butter, chopped shallots (*never* garlic, according to the French, hint, hint!), chopped parsley, and a little white wine. French, of course.

Everyone — even you, Pete — was stabbing the bits of meat with toothpicks and enjoying it immensely. When asked what the delicious dish was, all Red would say to anyone was, "Oh, just a little something I picked up in a neighborhood delicatessen. I don't remember the name of it, though," he lied, grinning to himself, but everyone *loved* it!

At 2030 hours [8:30 p.m.], Red turned up the radio that had softly been playing in the background (he didn't have a TV yet). *Your Hit Parade* was just coming on, sponsored by the company whose slogan was, *L.S.M.F.T. – Lucky Strikes Means Fine Tobacco*. You went back to the bedroom and returned with two packs of cigarettes. You lit up a Marlboro, and Davy lit up a Chesterfield. Such was the power of suggestion.

Aside from his duties as host, Red was just as busy pleasuring his guests as anyone else. You couldn't seem to take your eyes off him.

"You really like him, don't you, Pete?" Davy asked.

"Who?"

"Don't give me that shit! You know who I'm talking about. You haven't been able to take your eyes off of Red since we got here."

You smiled and took a deep breath as your eyes searched around the room until they found Red giving head to Pacheco's '*mushroom*'. "Yeah," you released the breath, still watching. "I do. Is it that obvious?"

"Yeah, but probably only to me," Davy said.

"And me," Alex said as he stepped up to the two of you, took the cigarettes out of your hands and dropped them in an almost empty glass of punch. He then pulled you guys into a three-way hug, which quickly became a three-way kiss with tongues darting in this mouth and then that mouth and back again and again. Three pair of hips were thrusting this way and that, banging the ever-hardening and lengthening ram-rods together. Six hands were roaming across backs and ass-cheeks, and fingers would occasionally probe where the sun don't shine.

You suddenly realized that Davy and Alex were locked in a passionate-sounding French kiss. You lowered your head and began sweeping your tongue back and forth across their nipples. After a bit, your tongue bath went lower and lower. Of course, both were shaven, so there was no 'treasure trail' to explore, but once on your knees, you managed to get at least their oozing heads in between your lips, and maybe a little more.

Their moans and groans grew louder, and each had a hand on one of your shoulders urging you on. "Suck it, baby." "Deeper, deeper, please." "Yeah, that's it. Getting' close." "Can't hold off much longer," you heard the two voices talking over each other. Moans and groans weren't just coming down to you from Davy and Alex; they were coming from all around you.

Suddenly, you could feel and taste the pulsing, throbbing spurting shots of liquid desserts from Davy and Alex, but you felt other hot, molten splats and dribbles across your naked back and in your hair. Soon, other tongues were licking *your* back; other hands, wet hands, were rubbing the back of *your* waist and *your* ass-cheeks. You swallowed the remnants of Davy's and Alex's gifts, and then you stood up.

You looked around, only to find that Red had not partaken in your 'ravishing shower of sperm, and the tongue cleansing'. Instead, he had merely watched.

Rollo turned and asked him, "Now that it's all gone, what *WAS* that tasty dark meat in the pan with the candle under it?"

"You really want to know?" Red answered with a question.

"Yeah!" "Yeah." "YEAH!" "It was delicious." "I loved it," came answers from the others.

"Escargot," he answered simply.

"What's that?" you asked.

"Snails," Red answered, looking around the room but not *at* anyone in particular.

There was total silence except for the radio. Then shock. And surprise — both good and bad. Rollo and Pacheco both threw their hands up to their mouths and ran to the bathroom, turning greener and greener as they went. It was their *thoughts* that made them sick, *not* the snails, but their own thoughts. Snails — French snails — prepared properly, are fantastically delicious, and they're not slimy at all!

Soon, everyone returned to the base. Everyone, that is, except for you and Red.

You needed to take a shower to get all that jizz out of your hair and off your back. Red offered to be of assistance. You accepted, thrilled that he would offer.

That weekend, between the showers and the bedroom activities, Red taught you everything he knew about male-to-male intimacy. There was not a thing that he gave, that he would not receive or accept himself. And before Monday morning came, the two of you had fallen in love. That should be capitalized. LOVE. With discussion, and knowing the male animal, you both agreed that *The family that plays together, stays together.* You both knew that the newness would someday wear off. You both knew that in all likelihood you'd lose your hot, trim, muscular bodies — in due time. You also knew that you'd have each other for as long as you both should live.

You playfully dried each other after the third shower that night, and then walked down the short hall to the disheveled bedroom filled with the smells and odors of masculine sex. Arms around each other, you kissed him on one of the several hickies you'd earlier inflicted on his neck, and you whispered into his ear... "I think this is the beginnin' of a beautiful friendship."

EPILOGUE

And that's the way it was.

And a beautiful friendship it was.

Your mornings were spent at the Base Hospital becoming acquainted with Orderlies' duties, with maintaining asepsis (freedom from infection or infectious conditions — not sterile, but extremely clean) for health safety of patients as well as hospital staff. Then, your afternoons were back to Seamanship Classes with Company 209, and your week-nights at the barracks.

Your weekends — all two of them — were spent with "Red", memorable, romantic, sex-filled weekends. You felt like your whole life had been empty of Love, of passion, and of *real* happiness. Never had you been happier before. You thought you were happy when you and Darkness were playing, working, exploring, and doing what young guys do, hanging together.

True, you loved Darkness, but as a brother born on the same day, and you loved Vashti, his mama, more'n ya did your own mama. But then, you *were* white, and he *was* black, and you knew that no matter how much you cared for each other, there could not be a deeper commitment or relationship during that day and age.

And in the *South*! Lordy! What would folks have said?

You knew damn good and well what folks would have said. At times, they still wore those chicken-shit, God-fearin' white hoods in that neck of the woods. He'd be tarred-and-feathered and probably burned to death. You'd be lynched or shackled and tied to a long rope attached to the back of a car, and drug across hill and dale till...??? If you were still alive after that, the good ol' boys would leave your torn and mangled body alone, out in the boondocks, or else they might just toss your body — conscious *or* unconscious; alive or not — into the gator-infested swamp. Just because that's the way it had always been done. And God help anybody who decided to be *different*.

Graduation day came. You were proud of yourself. Everyone in the Company was glad *that* day had finally come with orders to next duty stations.

Frank Moore and Jimmy Murphy, *happily*, were transferred to Yeoman School in Bainbridge, Maryland. A couple of years later you'd learned that they had been separated, Frank having been transferred to Incirlik Air Base in Turkey, and Jimmy having been sent to Guam, half a world apart.

Dick Wanker and Randy Strait were both ordered to the Seabees in Hawaii. They couldn't have been happier. You had a feeling that they didn't want to be split up.

Chakka Zzyzx shaped up nicely. He was awarded entrance into Officer Candidate School at Naval Station Newport, Rhode Island.

UN-officially, you heard the scuttlebutt that Petty Officer First Class Schlomo Schmuckatelli was found dead in a fire in his trashy office, on his stomach, his head toward the windows overlooking the Drill Field, his feet toward his desk. By the position of his belt and burned trousers, they had been hunkered around his ankles. There was no indication that he was wearing any underwear other than a studded, black leather, snap-on cock-ring. Popular opinion had it that ONI (Office of Naval Intelligence — an early precursor of NCIS) determined that he'd had a fatal heart attack while both sucking on a cigar and masturbating as he watched his Ceremonial Guardsmen rehearse their routines just one short week prior to the Graduation Ceremonies.

Charlie Dickens, bless his soul, went to school *somewhere* to become a Recruiting Officer.

Hank Snow and Byron Sweetwater, too, were separated. Hank was ordered to Naval Air Station Keflavik in Iceland (a fitting place for someone named *Snow*), to become an Air Traffic Controller. And Byron was ordered to USNTC San Diego to eventually become a Company Commander.

Another breakup was Rollo Burnside and Pacheco Keskeskeck. Rollo was ordered to Sea Duty on an Aircraft Carrier and he became a Cook, one of the most loved or most hated people on a ship. Oh, they could be bastards sometimes, with all that Saltpeter!

And you learned that Pacheco had been sent to Radioman School and then ordered to Sea Duty aboard a Submarine out of Naval Station Newport. He discovered that he was claustrophobic, contrary to all the tests he underwent before his assignment. He *hated* being closed in all the time, and *UNDERWATER* at that! He'd asked for a transfer, but his Captain refused his request; he was just too damned good. Well, Pacheco decided to take matters into his own hands… *literally*!

He jacked-off in front of his bunkmates or in the showers or in the Engine Room. He openly offered up his mouth or his ass to anyone, anytime. Even his Captain, the Commanding Officer of the Submarine. He started tying his shirttails together just under his muscular tits, exposing his dark brown, smooth, hairless Latin-slash-Native American midriff. He walked the narrow, tight passageways with a swish to his hips. And finally, after being under the northern ice-cap for a couple of weeks, one day, in front of about twenty officers and other sailors, he fell to his knees in front of the *surprised* 2nd in Command — the Lt. JG (Lieutenant Junior Grade). He grabbed the officer by his hips, and thrust his gaping mouth onto the uniform-covered fire-hose-like piece of tube-steak hanging down his left thigh. He laved his saliva-wet tongue up and down the monster, leaving a dark gray, wet, stain on the leg of the khaki trousers.

Well, to make a long story short, as soon as the Sub returned to NS Newport, Pacheco Keskeskeck was court-martialed out of the US Navy for being a *"security risk"* who was susceptible to being blackmailed. Yeah, right. If he weren't ashamed of, or embarrassed about being a *cocksucker* or *fudge-packer*, how could he be blackmailed?

And Slick O'Hoolihan – Ass Kicker and his four hooligans? Well, Slick and three of his sidekicks just couldn't make it, even in a different Company of Recruits. All four of them were kicked out with Bad Conduct Discharges, before they got out of the Brig.

But the fifth one — Arlo Kormann — the shy, timid one who was quiet and hung his head when the SPs came aboard the bus that first day you arrived at USNTC — he, too, was eventually ordered to Navy Hospital Corpsman School there at Great Lakes, and became a junior Corpsman to *your* rating, Pete. You quickly took him under your own wing, just as Red had taken you under his.

Yes, Red had recently re-enlisted for another six years (with a good re-enlistment bonus, I might add), and you had signed on for four years. You finished Corpsman School and, as expected — with a little influence to the Commandant of the Base from CPO David N. Jones — were stationed at Great Lakes Hospital.

You and Red loved the military. And you loved each other. You just hoped and prayed that you could always be stationed together. It didn't matter where. Timbuktu, Antarctica, the Pentagon, aboard an Aircraft Carrier or even that newfangled '*nucular*' [7] Sub, *The Nautilus*.

Oh, yes! I almost forgot about Alex. That's Floyd Reginald Alexander Peabody the Third, I mean. You remember him, don't you, Petey? Of course you do. Just teasing.

You and Red spent at *least* one weekend a month with him and CPO Davy Jones. Either at the old fixer-upper of a secluded, clapboard-covered farmhouse y'all had found on twenty-seven wooded acres of land about midway between Great Lakes NTC and Rockford, Illinois. And then Davy and Alex bought the big ol' dilapidated barn from you, had it torn down, reassembled, and turned it into what the Yankees might call an open, airy, loft, with a huge fireplace, open on all sides.

Oh, those were happy days when you were together as two separate couples, or when you were together hunting, fishing, camping, swimming, boating, ice skating, or romping together as a happy foursome. Oh! And those 'hangar parties'! They went on, at least twice a year, for many years.

I gotta question for you, though. Did you ever find out what Davy's middle initial, 'N', stood for? I've always known, but he'd sworn me to secrecy.

Yeah, that's right, Neptune, the Roman god of water and the sea. Davy had a powerful ally in his middle name, and the god surrounded him with those who would love him, and whom he could love in return. You came close, Pete, but Alex, that's right, Floyd Reginald Alexander Peabody III, was his soulmate. They became equal partners in every way, both giving and receiving equally, alone with each other, or with others, they were physically, mentally, emotionally, and spiritually *ONE* just like Fred Johnson and you, Peters Balzak Dix 5-Oh-9. Just like you.

Live long and be prosperous and happy.
That's the way your 'Red' would want it.
The End.

FOOTNOTES

1. Phallocampsis = Curvature of the penis when erect [according to <u>Dorland's Pocket Medical Dictionary, 1960</u>], whether interfering with intercoursal ability or not, and whether or not it is painful to the man afflicted by the condition.

2. Saltpeter = http://www.snopes.com/military/saltpeter.asp

3. Bosun's Punch = Newbies on board ship for the first time are often told to find this phony tool in one of the ship's Bosun's (Boatswain's) offices. The Bosun himself PUNCHES the newbie in the shoulder for not knowing better.

4. Rain locker = a shower aboard ship

5. Slang = http://en.wiktionary.org/wiki/Appendix:Glossary_of_U.S._Navy_slang

6. NUB (pronounced 'NOOB') = New Useless Body, *et al*. Term referred to newly reported sailors with no qualifications or experience. Usually tasked with dirty and nasty jobs often referred to as 'Shit Work'.

7   '*nucular*' = MIS-pronunciation of the word 'nuclear'. The *Free Dictionary* says that "U.S. presidents Dwight D. Eisenhower, Bill Clinton, and George W. Bush have all used this pronunciation."

ABOUT THE AUTHOR

Since his landlubber's engagement with the U.S.Navy, *El Aurens* has been a Jack-of-all-trades, Master-of-none. Surgical Technician, Pharmacy Technician, and Embalmer. Overhead Sprinkler Engineer for fire insurance. Hotel owner and operator. Community Theatre produced-Playwright, Actor, Director, and Stage Manager. Editor and Grammarian for several other authors. Was published in national newspapers while yet in high school, and in the internationally recognized slick *Palm Springs Life Magazine* in the early 1970s. Has lived for a time in Canada, Mexico, Haiti, Ecuador,  Peru, and Egypt. Now retired in the South-west, and has been writing professionally for the past four years.